## DATE DUE

| JAN 1 4 2007 | | |
|---|---|---|
| OCT 0 6 2007 | | |
| OCT 1 3 2007 | | |
| JUL 2 9 2008 | | |
| | | |
| | | |
| | | |
| | | |
| | | |
| | | |
| | | |
| | | |
| | | |
| | | |
| | | |
| | | |

Demco, Inc. 38-293

# Year Walk

# Year Walk

## ANN NOLAN CLARK

The Viking Press
New York

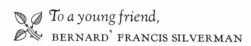 *To a young friend,*
BERNARD' FRANCIS SILVERMAN

FIRST EDITION

Copyright © 1975 by Ann Nolan Clark
All rights reserved
First published in 1975 by The Viking Press, Inc.
625 Madison Avenue, New York, N.Y. 10022
Published simultaneously in Canada by
The Macmillan Company of Canada Limited

PRINTED IN U.S.A.

1   2   3   4   5   79   78   77   76   75

Library of Congress Cataloging in Publication Data
Clark, Ann Nolan, 1898–   Year walk.
SUMMARY: In 1910 a sixteen-year-old boy from the
Spanish-Basque country comes to Idaho to help his
godfather herd sheep across the Northwest frontier.
[1. Shepherds—Fiction.      2. The West—Fiction]
Title PZ7.C5296Ye      [Fic]      74—23565
ISBN 0-670-79367-1

(TO THE READER) When I was a young girl driving with my father—and then at a much later date with my son—in the rangeland and the foothills of New Mexico, I always had a special feeling for the lonely campsite, the campfire, the tent or the sheep wagon, the hobbled mule, the dog guarding the sheep, and sometimes the herder himself whom we saw in the distance, always near but never close to the deep-rutted sandy road we traveled.

They were Basque herders, my father told me, forever at war with the cowboys whose cattle herds also grazed the rangeland and drank at the infrequent springs and waterholes. The cattle herds were always running. The cowboys were riding top speed on their well-trained horses, but the herders walked by themselves with their sheep, their pack mules, and their dogs. Even in those days I wanted to write their story.

That was a long time ago; quite a few years and quite a few books for a story to wait to get itself written.

At last, four years ago, a friend and I went to Spain to have a look at the Spanish Basque land where these herders have come from, but even then an Irish book wedged itself between the Basque story and me. Two years ago the time had come; the

Basque would be the next book to be written. Another friend went with me to Spain to really get to know the homeland and the home people of our American Basque. In America we were told, "Basque people do not like strangers. It will be impossible to get to know them." Yet we found the Spanish Basques a very friendly people. They took us where we wanted to go. They showed us what we wanted to see. They told us what we needed to know. I will never forget my visit with a Basque family in an ancient *caserío* in the Pyrenees Basque land of Spain. It was like the one my Kepa, later, was to live in.

When I came home again there was reading to do. I cannot understand why there are not nearly enough books written about Basques. To me they are a fascinating people with a history predating Rome and a language the oldest in Europe. But my librarian friends came forth to help me: Virginia Hanson of Utah; Lutie Higby of the University of Arizona library in Tucson, Arizona. The University library at Las Vegas, Nevada, and the Library of Congress found published and unpublished dissertations on Basque history and traditions, culture, and language. There were also the few Basque books in English and English translations.

Carna McDowell, of Utah, and Robert Laxalt, of the University of Las Vegas, told me of their fathers' experiences as early herdsmen in Utah and Nevada. Boyd Sawyer's book *Nevada Nomads* was helpful. After a year's reading I was ready for Idaho, the sheep country I had chosen to write about.

At this point Dorothy and Basil Aldecoa and Carmen and Joe Letc of Boise, Idaho, could not have been more helpful. They took me to their sheep ranch at lambing and shearing time, and later in the year we caught up with the herders, their dogs, their mules, and the sheep.

I do not know Big Smoky in Idaho, but I know the mountain regions of New Mexico, Colorado, and the foothills of Utah like, as the Spanish say, "the palm of my hand." The Idaho forestry office nearby answered what questions I had.

Two years had gone by before I started the book itself, but the writing was easy and the book was finished.

New Mexico, Utah, Nevada, and Idaho have given bits of Basque history, traditions, and dreams to enrich this book. I hope the story will remind young American Basque readers that their ancestors made the trails and walked them, grazed the wilderness, homesteaded the rangeland, and had a great share in opening the American Southwest.

A. N. C.

# Contents

# CHARACTERS IN THE BOOK

KEPA'S FAMILY

FATHER

MOTHER

MANUEL, *oldest—does not want to inherit the land, is a teacher in the village*

CARMEN—*who is to inherit the land*

LUISA—*who breaks tradition by marrying a man of a neighboring valley.*

MARÍA—*was to have married Diego, who enlisted in the Spanish Army and was killed; later she marries his brother José (a European custom)*

KEPA—*Pedro's namesake and godson*

FIRST NEIGHBOR'S FAMILY

JOSÉ, *oldest—inherits the land*

PEDRO—*Kepa's godfather, who has gone to America and marries a French Basque*

DIEGO—*enlisted in the Spanish Army and was killed; had been betrothed to María*

PACO—*youngest, and a priest in the village*

AMERICAN FAMILY

PEDRO

WIFE, *a French Basque*

MARÍA CRISTINA

ANTONIO } *the twins*
TOMÁS

1st Part

# THE TRAIL'S BEGINNING

1 BOISE! KEPA THOUGHT, Boise in Idaho, America! The young boy jumped down from the high step of the railway car carefully carrying his portmanteau, his guitar, his shepherd's staff.

The engine whistled and puffed steam noisily; the train jerked and began to move along the track. Faces filled the open windows of the passenger cars. Arms waved good-byes. Voices called out messages to the boy on the station platform, but there was only one voice he understood. A voice calling in Basque, "As soon as I learn how to drive the automobile, Kepa, I'll come to see you every Sunday." The voice belonged to Kepa's friend Alejandro, who was from their home village in the Pyrenees mountains of the Basque country in Spain.

The boys had left the village together, crossed the wild Atlantic and the wide American land together, but now they were parting. They had not planned to part, but Alejandro's ticket read "California." Kepa watched the departing train. Alejandro's voice kept ringing in his ears. He had not answered. He could find no words. His friend was gone.

Homesickness as sharp as pain engulfed him. He saw again, as plainly as if he had been there, his homeland in Spain instead of the almost empty station platform in a strange and unknown place. He saw again the rocky, narrow mountain stream that divided the *caserío* of the two families—his father's and First Neighbor's. He saw the rolling hills and the towering peaks of the Pyrenees encircling the valley. The trees of the hill—beech, chestnut, and oak—came to the edges of the cornfields divided by the mountain stream. The vineyards lay between the fields and the meadow pastures, which were dotted by ricks of bracken and high grass-wrapped poles wearing rain hats and looking like tall, awkward giants. He saw again the two old three-story whitewashed stone *caseríos,* with wooden balconies at the middle-story windows, standing each in its own land on its own side of the river.

His memories were broken by the sound of someone softly calling his name, "Kepa, Kepa."

The boy turned. The man who had spoken to him was wearing leather boots, not rope-soled shoes, a big hat instead of a beret, but otherwise he looked as Kepa remembered him, a tall, leanly built, quiet man, reliable and kind. With him was a very pretty girl. Basque, Kepa thought, and yet not Basque, more independent looking than Basque girls in Spain. He corrected himself. Not more independent—his sisters were independent. Perhaps the word was free. Could a person show freedom, he wondered.

"Kepa," the man said again, walking toward the boy.

"Godfather Pedro," Kepa answered shyly.

"Your godfather, none other. Second son of your father's First Neighbor and the man you were named for, young fellow," Pedro declared, shaking the boy's hand, pummeling his shoulders. There was no mistaking his welcome. Kepa felt taken into the man's heart, his family, his country; homesickness left him. "You seem to have made a trainload of American friends." Pedro laughed, looking at the departing train, now only a speck in the distance. "Do you speak English to make American friends so quickly?" "No," Kepa answered, "and at first they were not my friends. They laughed at Alejandro and me." Then he added, "Alejandro is the postmaster's son in our village. Remember him?"

"No," Pedro said, "but I remember his father. Where is Alejandro going?"

Kepa also was looking at the departing train. "To his uncle in California, America, to learn to be a mechanic to fix the American automobiles. He will come here every Sunday to play *pelota* with me as we did in Spain. Your brother José gave me his *pelota* ball and mitt so I could bring them to America and play *pelota* here."

Kepa did not know that his godfather was thinking, How can I answer the boy? How can I tell him that probably he will never see his friend again? How can I explain the bigness of America? America is too big. Too big to learn to take without a lot of pain. Abruptly, Pedro turned to the pretty girl beside him and said to Kepa, "Remember my daughter? She was with me when I visited the Basque country. Remember?"

Kepa nodded. He remembered her. She had been a nuisance, tagging along with him everywhere he went. He also remembered his manners. "María Cristina, at your service," he said in formal Spanish.

She answered him in Basque, "Not María Cristina, but Chris, spelled with an *h* in it, the American way." The girl's words were Basque but her voice and manner were American.

Kepa could not hide his surprise. "You are American," he blurted in amazement.

She answered looking straight into his eyes, "Basque American." Then she repeated, for emphasis, "*Basque American*." Kepa wondered if he liked her. He thought, perhaps, he didn't.

"I see you brought your shepherd's staff. Good. I think you will make a fine herder," Pedro said as they loaded Kepa's staff, his guitar, and his portmanteau in the trunk of the car. Kepa was pleased, but also, looking at the shiny, big automobile, he

5

thought of Alejandro and had a moment of pain for the loss of a friend.

"We'll drop Chris off here at her school," Pedro explained, stopping before a large building. "She was excused from classes this morning to come to the station to meet you," and to Chris he said, "I'll come back for you and the twins late this afternoon when I bring your mother home from the ranch."

Kepa was all eyes. "Do they have a school in that palace?"

Pedro laughed. "It isn't a palace, although it's big enough for one. It's a school and full of children. The twins go there, also." After a moment he added, "Next year Chris will be in high school, and she will go to a different building." They rode on in silence.

Kepa looked at the streets of Boise, at the houses in rows, smaller and closer together than the houses of Spain. There was something here that he liked, a cleanness and a freshness that one could feel and smell. The boy felt that he had never smelled air before so fresh and clean and dry. It had a buoyancy that made him feel light-headed and lighthearted. The sun too seemed different here than in the mountains of the Pyrenees. It was so bright, so dazzling, and it warmed without taking away the cool crispness of the early spring day.

"Perhaps she will go away to college." Godfather was still thinking of his daughter. "But I doubt it," he continued. "She is the real sheepman of the family and never wants to be away from the ranch for long. The twins—I don't know what the twins want. This year they say doctors. Last year they wanted to go to sea in ships."

The man looked at the boy sitting so quietly beside him. He looks like I did when I first came to America, he thought, eager and hopeful, frightened and homesick. Aloud he said, "This is a great day for me. I have been waiting for this day since the time you were born when I asked your father if I could be your godfather and you my namesake. As long ago as that I had

6

planned to come to America and to send for you when I could."

"I know," Kepa told him. "When you came for a visit you said that when I was sixteen and the year was 1910 you would send for me."

Pedro was surprised. "That was at least four years ago and you remember it?" he asked.

"Five years ago," Kepa corrected him, "and I remembered every day!"

"Do you remember what happened when your father received my letter asking for you?" Pedro asked curiously. Kepa laughed. He would never forget what happened.

The letter had come. He had stood in the wide double Dutch door of his father's house watching his friend Alejandro walk up the trail from the village below. Alejandro held the letter carefully; to deliver it in good condition was his responsibility. Kepa and the village boy were about the same size, the same stocky build, the same age, and wore the same kind of clothing: baggy pants, short pleated coats, and dark berets. They looked alike for they were Basque, and Basque the world over look alike.

Kepa called out a cheerful Basque greeting and Alejandro returned it, adding proudly, "I bring a letter. It is for your father."

Kepa and his father had been forking fern and mint into the stable to bed down the cow and the donkey, which were stabled in the ground-floor portion of the ancient farmhouse. Now the older man came to the doorway to greet the boy and receive the letter he had brought. Father looked at the stamp-covered envelope, turning it over and over in his work-hardened hands. Kepa's mother and sisters, Carmen and María, came out on the kitchen balcony above the double Dutch doors and peered down at the village boy and Father as he examined the letter. Kepa, also, watched his father. He had been certain at first sight of the letter that it had come from Godfather Pedro who lived in Idaho, America. It is from him, he thought. I know it is.

7

At last Father opened the letter and read it slowly. Then he slowly and carefully returned it to the envelope and stood for a time gazing at the surrounding hills and the high peaks towering behind them. When he had thought of the exact words he wanted to say he turned to the village boy. "Tell your father I thank him for sending me my letter and you, also, for bringing it." The boy turned to go, but Father stopped him. "Wait," he said, "I, too, have messages for you to deliver. Go to my daughter Luisa, who lives with her husband in Upper Valley, and to the village below to my son Manuel, the schoolteacher, and to Padre Paco, the youngest son of First Neighbor. Go, also, to the old herder on the mountaintop, who is neither kin nor neighbor, but who has served my family well and therefore is part of it. Tell each of them to come here to my *caserío* a week from today to discuss a matter of great importance to this family. I, myself, will tell the members of my household and also José, eldest son of First Neighbor. Do you understand the message and the names of those who will receive it?"

The boy nodded and Father returned to his work, saying to Kepa, "Discussion will take place when the time comes for discussion. Today's work will be done now, today."

Carmen came running down the wide, steep stone stairway that led to the family living quarters on the middle story. Breathlessly, she called to Alejandro to stop for a bowl of soup before returning to the village. Kepa would have liked to have gone with Alejandro up to his mother's bright, sweet-smelling *casina*, her kitchen, for he knew that as surely as his mother's soup had salt she and her daughter Carmen would question the boy about the letter he had given Father. Kepa looked up at the kitchen balcony longingly, but his father had spoken, and when his father spoke he expected to be obeyed. Reluctantly the boy went inside to fork the fern and mint leaves from the cart into clean bed downs for the animals.

8

2 THE DAYS THAT FOLLOWED seemed as long to Kepa as the years had been that he had waited for the letter to come. They were not quiet days. Mother and her two daughters swept and scrubbed and cooked and whispered together. The letter had come from America, from Idaho, America—that much the village boy had told them.

"It's from Pedro. I know it's from Pedro," Carmen said.

"Why does he write to your father?" Mother asked.

"We will know at the meeting," Carmen told her.

"But what is it we are to know?" Mother worried, scrubbing the floor a second time.

"What is it we are to know?" Carmen repeated, sweeping the stone steps in a flurry of action. "I think we know."

José, eldest son of First Neighbor, had inherited the family *caserío* and thus the house, the pasture, the fields and garden, and the vineyard were his by unbreakable tradition. This being so, Pedro, the second son, had gone to America to find a new life there. After almost ten years a return visit to his homeplace had proven that he had found a fruitful one, having a beautiful wife, a young daughter, twin sons, and money in his pocket.

"Pedro is Kepa's godfather and namesake," Carmen reminded

9

her younger sister. "You know the Basque way as well as I do, a never-ending chain of helping hands." María did not answer. What she thought no one ever knew.

Father was the only serene one in his family, going about his work calmly, doing every day the chores of the day. Kepa worked beside him as usual, but now their days were not made brighter by their shared laughter or sweeter by their talk. They worked silently. If Father had some secret knowledge, he did not tell what it was. If he had some nagging worry, he did not show it. He seemed interested in the task of the moment. Kepa, too, was quiet, lost in his own deep thoughts.

The boy knew that Father's letter was from Idaho in faraway America, for he had heard Alejandro speak of it to his mother and his sisters. That being true, he knew it must be from his godfather, Pedro. He hoped the letter contained the fulfillment of the promise that had been made to him, and a request to his family. What his family's answer to the request would be was not to his knowing. In the Basque country, before any decision is made it is discussed first by every member of the family and every member of First Neighbor's family, who are as close as kin. Even those who work for the family are asked to give an opinion, and all opinions are listened to with respect and receive thoughtful consideration. Father, Kepa knew, would give the final word. He was the authority; this was his right, but he would arrive at the final decision by weighing carefully the combined opinions of the group. Kepa remembered other family discussions. He was the youngest of both families and had been a part of all family problems and their solutions. No one could know in advance what might happen. The boy's days were torn by hope and doubt. His nights were heavy with dreams, both good and bad. The days dragged on—dragged on. But each day passed, and at last the long week was ended. The day for the conference had come.

Father sat at the head of the long hand-carved table in the *sala*, the special room that was used only for special occasions. Down the length of the table, each in his rightful place, sat the members of his family, the members of First Neighbor's family, and the old, old shepherd of the mountaintop, each one dear to Father's heart and held lovingly in his esteem.

On festive occasions, Kepa thought, the *sala* seemed a brighter place; today its mood seemed serious and somber. The room was spacious and high-ceilinged, but now shadows lurked in the corners and seemed to draw the walls closer together. The massive hand-hewn oak beams spanning its width made the ceiling seem lower. High on the whitewashed walls hung framed pictures of family members of other days. Kepa looked up at them hoping for a friendly smile, but the pictured faces were without feeling and the eyes stared at nothing. Kepa looked down at the wide plank floor that had been whitened by years of diligent scrubbing and wondered how many feet had walked across it to the heavy, high table where now his family sat. The hand-carved chests placed stiffly around the walls were heavy and dark, and the thin lines of sunshine streaking through the narrow windows neither lightened nor brightened the room.

The dark suits and berets of the men and the long black aprons of the women added to the heavy feeling that lay in the pit of Kepa's stomach. The boy knew that what each one said in this room, at this table today, would be frank, thoughtful, deliberate, and each word would be counted and weighed, to make the final decision.

Father, patriarch of the family, brought out the letter. He unfolded it with care, read it slowly, silently forming each word with his lips. His actions stated plainly that the contents of this letter were not to be shared hastily or thoughtlessly. The hushed stillness of the people around the table was electric with suspense.

Kepa's mouth was dry; his hands were wet and clammy. He looked at no one.

Finally, Father returned the letter to its envelope and the envelope to his pocket. Nodding to José, eldest son of First Neighbor, he said, "This letter is from your brother Pedro, second son of your parents, may their souls rest in peace." Then looking at Kepa, he added, "It concerns our youngest son Pedro, the boy we call Kepa."

Kepa sat hunched in his chair at the foot of the table, all eyes and ears, but hoping he had made himself invisible. Father ignored him and continued talking, looking around the table at each member in turn. "As you know, José inherited the land, and Pedro went to America where it is said gold pieces lay scattered over the ground waiting for those who come to gather them." The people seated at the table nodded in agreement. America, they had heard, was truly a land of gold.

Father said, gesturing toward Mother who sat at his right, "Sometime before Pedro left us, our Kepa was born, a lusty, squalling red-faced creature as I recall." There was a whisper of laughter around the table. "Pedro asked us," Father continued, "if the boy could be his namesake and godson, a privilege we were proud to give." Father again glanced at Kepa, and Kepa again tried to make himself smaller in the shelter of his chair. "In this letter," Father said, tapping the pocket where he had placed it, "which Pedro writes me, he states that at last, having acquired both money and sheep, he is able to assume his duty as godfather to our son."

Everyone at the table had thought that the letter was from Pedro and had guessed what probably he had written, but now that Father had said it in words, the surmise became fact. Everyone looked at Kepa in surprise as if they had not seen him since he had been a red-faced baby.

"The years go so slowly," the old shepherd mumbled, "one

cannot trace them, and so fast one is confronted only with what they have done."

Kepa clenched his hands under the table edge so no one could see their trembling. He must act neither embarrassed nor afraid. Steadily he made his gaze travel around the table, look-ing, momentarily, at each person in turn. Ten other people and all more important than he was, because they were older. This was his test. He did not flinch. Steadily he told them, "I am fifteen years old, going on sixteen. Almost ready to become a man."

There was silence around the table.

3 FATHER BEGAN TO TALK AGAIN. "Pedro has sent the passage money for Kepa to go to America. He writes that he will pay the boy money to herd the sheep." Father paused. There was silence. Then he added, "Pedro writes that he himself was fifteen, almost sixteen, when he went to America. He says he believes it is a good age for our Kepa to go." Father glanced briefly at his youngest son, then looked at the others. "I would like your thoughts on this matter," he said, passing the *bota* for each one to fill his mug.

Padre Paco, although First Neighbor's youngest son, was a man of the church, so it was fitting that he be first to speak. "Kepa is a good boy," he said thoughtfully. "I have given him strict instruction in our ways. It may be well that he take these old and strong Basque beliefs to the new country of America." There was a murmur around the table. "Our Kepa is a good boy. You have taught him well."

Manuel, schoolteacher in the village and firstborn of Father's household, spoke next. "The young Pedro—Kepa as we call him—is well educated. He has been five years at school and can speak, read, and write Spanish and French, and, of course, our Basque tongue. In America, he will bring honor to our house

14

as well as to our Basque country." Again there was a murmur of agreement. "Our Kepa has book learning. You have taught him much. He would do well in America."

"Honor to both our houses," José said distinctly. Then, being a practical man who thought that money was as necessary as church and school, he added, "And also money. As you may remember, when Pedro came back to visit us five years ago, he had money enough to reroof my house with slate." Then he proudly added, "A slate roof is not bought for nothing."

"Money is needed in our poor country," Carmen said sadly. She was the second child and oldest daughter, who had been chosen to inherit the homeplace. "Kepa should go to America and come back quickly with money in his pocket to help all of us. Although I am not certain how long this house can wait to be reroofed with slate."

Luisa, younger sister of Carmen, spoke smugly. "My husband's home is well built. It does not need a new slate roof." Luisa, a year ago, had caused family displeasure by marrying a young man from another valley and she was always eager to show how right she had been in her choice of a young man to marry.

Father was displeased with both of his daughters. To Carmen he said, "This house, which in time will be yours, has withstood the storms of winter for two hundred years and will withstand them for a hundred more." To Luisa, "Your husband's house I am sure is greatly respected in your husband's valley. What would be thought of it in this valley I cannot say."

María, youngest daughter, who was to have married Diego, third son of First Neighbor, said nothing, but no one expected her to speak her thoughts. Since the day that was to have been her wedding day became instead her day of heartbreak, she seldom spoke.

The old shepherd coughed as prelude to his talk, which was

the last and also the longest. "To herd sheep in America—that is a dream few of us have seen come true. It was my dream once, but it remained only a dream. I remember when gold was discovered in California, America. It was at that time that our first young Basque went to the new country. They went to find gold." The Old One wiped tears from his eyes before he continued. "Kepa is a good shepherd. For the last three summers he has herded the sheep in the meadow of my mountains. He has herded many sheep, not only the nine belonging to his father but with them the eleven that José owns. Let him take this knowledge to America."

All had spoken, the sons and daughters of Father's household, the sons of First Neighbor, and the loved and respected old shepherd. There was one person, Mother, who had not spoken, but always she had put the welfare of her children first. Their welfare was more important to her than the tears of her heart. Kepa's welfare would be more important now, her family thought, and although he was her youngest—and for that reason her dearest—she would let him go.

Father smiled around the table with affection and approval. Then he turned to his wife. "All but our Little Mother have shared their thoughts on this grave matter," he told them. "When she joins us in agreement, then Teacher Manuel may write the letter to Pedro telling him that we are sending his godson to him."

For the first time Kepa dared to believe that he would be permitted to go. He had dreamed of it for so long, since the day his godfather had told him, "I was almost sixteen when I went. When you are that age, I will send for you. It is a hard life, but you are Basque. A Basque can endure. You will learn to like it."

Kepa had been too young to remember Pedro when he went away to America, but he remembered his coming back for a visit five years ago. Pedro had brought his wife and a daughter, who had been about eight at the time, and two younger boys. Kepa

16

had been too shy to talk to the beautiful young wife, and the little girl and her brothers had been a nuisance. But what had been important to him was the gold watch Godfather Pedro kept in his pocket. A gold watch! For years Kepa had dreamed of the day he would go to America and buy a gold watch. Now that he was really going, Kepa thought, it would be no time at all until he would have money in his hand and a gold watch in his pocket. Kepa smiled to himself. He could almost hear the gold watch ticking.

Suddenly the boy's daydream was shattered. His mother was speaking in a voice as calm and everyday-sounding as if she were saying, "Come eat—the soup is hot." But there was no kinship between her voice and her words. Kepa heard her saying, "My youngest son is not going to Idaho, America. I do not permit it." Each word dropped upon his ears as a heavy stone dropping into his heart.

Silence blanketed the room and the people. No one spoke or moved or seemed to breathe. All eyes were turned toward Mother, not in disapproval, but in disbelief. Every day of their lives she had been Little Mother to all of them, understanding their problems, helping them in troubled times, loving them for their sins as much as for their virtues. As long as they could remember, Little Mother had been on their side, had backed what they wanted to do, had tilted the scales in their favor. Now all eyes were turned toward her, all silently asking, "Why? Why do you do this, Little Mother? Why?"

At last Father broke the heavy silence. "Deep thought often corrects its own mistakes," he said mildly. "Next week we will meet again to end this matter in complete agreement, as is our way. Until then, go in peace." Father placed his hand lovingly on Mother's shoulder. Together they left the room.

Outside, an autumn wind with a promise of first snow rippled over the tree-covered hills, swaying the blood-red bracken and pushing against the bushes heavy with berries that bordered the narrow trail down the mountainside. Tinka, the great Pyrenees dog—"mat dog" he was called because he always slept on a mat outside the wide Dutch doors—growled faintly in his sleep, perhaps dreaming of the old days when he was guard dog of the old house in the valley.

From the great house to the village below on a still day was a four-hour journey on foot. It would take longer today fighting the wind and menaced by the coming darkness. Luisa and her husband did not have so far to go to their *caserío* in the Upper Valley, but their trail was not as well traveled as the one to the village, and their walking time would be as long. None of them minded cold nor wind nor walking on a mountain trail. They were Basque, sturdy mountain people whose history was old when Rome was young. Through the centuries being Basque had been their strength and their shield.

The old shepherd, whose leaving Mother would not permit, planned to stay the week to be present at the second meeting. Now he went with Kepa and the dog, Tinka, to herd the sheep from their day pasture to their night bed with the other animals. They had to herd José's sheep the long way home across the narrow footbridge that spanned the mountain river, for Kepa knew the stubborn animals would refuse to wade through the shallow stream. Kepa was glad for the Old One's company, and when they parted for the night the shepherd told him, "Work of the day dulls the pain of the day, and the darkness of night brings the balm of sleep." The boy thought as he so often did when the shepherd talked to him that the old herder's words seemed to bring with them the coolness and the quiet healing of his mountaintop world. The boy wondered why there seemed to be a bond between places and people. This, perhaps, he thought, was the reason why the name of a Basque homeplace gave the owner his surname. Thinking such thoughts kept his mind busy until sleep finally came to ease the hurt of the day's disappointment.

18

4 KEPA'S THOUGHTS WERE BROKEN by his godfather's teasing voice, "Come back to America, Kepa. Your memory has been taking you to Spain. What happened when Father received my letter? Did he call a family meeting?"

The boy looked at his godfather. What he said was true. His memories had taken him to Spain, but he was now here, in America, where he wanted to be, and he was sitting beside his godfather. He wanted to talk to him. He wanted to tell him about that day and the week that followed, but he could not sort the pictures that were racing through his mind into simple sentences. Finally, he managed to say, "Yes, Father called the family together."

Pedro laughed. "You don't want to tell me that your father was against your coming but the Little Mother was for it."

"No," Kepa said sadly, "Father was for it. The Little Mother said no."

Pedro stopped the car. This was where he wanted to come anyway, he thought, glancing at the store in front of him. Then he turned to Kepa. "But the Little Mother was always for what we wanted to do. The family members may have had other ideas, but not Little Mother. What happened?"

Again Kepa's memories took him back to the *sala* of his father's *caserío*. Again he saw the members of his family in his mother's kitchen eating the food Mother had prepared for them, knowing in her heart that snow would not keep them from coming. They were here as they had been a week ago, eating, talking, laughing together in the Basque way of living each minute for its own delight. Yet under their gaiety ran a concern as water sometimes runs under a crystal glaze of ice.

All too soon they followed Father into the *sala* and seated themselves in their places, Mother on Father's right, Padre Paco on Father's left, and Kepa, the youngest, at the foot of the table. The *bota* was passed around, each person filling his mug, sipping his drink, and looking at Father.

Father broke the silence because it was his duty to be the first to speak although, this time, it was not his pleasure. "Now that we have come together again to discuss this family matter of importance, who will be the first to say what is in his mind?" He looked at Mother who was looking down at her small, work-worn hands, clenched tightly in the folds of her apron.

But it was Kepa who answered his father. Clearly, calmly, he answered in a voice that showed neither fear nor embarrassment. "My Father, with your permission, I will be the first to speak."

The boy's father, his sisters, José, the old shepherd looked at him in amazement. The surprised look on their faces said as plainly as words, "This is not our small Kepa speaking; here speaks a boy on the threshold of manhood." The padre and the maestro looked at him not with surprise, but with respect, thinking, He is a good pupil. He is responding to our good teaching.

His mother gave him a long and loving look and lovingly he returned her gaze, speaking now directly to her. "My Mother, since you do not permit me to go to America, and, of course, I cannot go without your permission, Paco, our padre, and Manuel, my teacher-brother, have told me they will show me how to fill out the forms to enlist in the Army of Spain."

There was a cry from María, the silent one. "Not the Spanish Army! Never the Spanish Army. Diego enlisted, and what happened? He was killed in battle." María began to sob.

Mother spoke to the others, "Permit María to cry. She has had no tears since Diego's death. Let her tears fall to wash clean the bitterness in her heart." The little woman looked around the table. "You cry, also. I see tears on your cheeks. Cry then, all of you, but cry with María for Diego. Do not cry with me for Kepa. My Kepa will not enlist in the Spanish Army. Why should he, I ask you. Why should he?"

Manuel answered, "Because it is the law. If Kepa had gone to America, the Spanish Government would have permitted us to pay a price for his not enlisting. But since he is staying in Spain he must enlist in the Army of Spain. This is the law." Kepa watched his mother. Manuel had not convinced her.

"He is not old enough to enlist," she answered. "It will be years before the Army can take him." Mother shrugged. "Who knows what may happen years from now?"

Again Manuel was the one to answer her. "Not years, Little Mother. Remember, by Spanish reckoning, when one has had his sixteenth birthday, he is counted as being in his seventeenth year. Kepa's sixteenth birthday is almost here. A year from now he will be in his eighteenth year, a good age for the Army. The time for enlistment for Kepa is only a step beyond the next turn in his trail."

Paco leaned across the table toward Mother to emphasize what he had to say. "The boy has no land nor calling for the church or for teaching. You forbid his going to America. What is left but the Army?"

Luisa felt it was her turn to speak. She did not dare go against her mother's wishes by saying, "Permit him to go to America," so she tried another tack. "We sent my husband's youngest brother Juan to America," she said.

Carmen, as always, flamed at her sister's words. "In your husband's valley you had the money, perhaps, to pay the Spanish Government their fee to release your husband's brother from Army service. In our poor valley, money does not grow on the trees."

Manuel jumped to his feet, but Mother spoke first, "Since when do we not have money to pay for whatever it is our children need?" Manuel outshouted his mother. "I have the money. I will pay it. Your husband's brother, Luisa, is not the only one whose family can have the money, as my mother tells you, to pay for the needs of its children. My mother has it. I give it to her."

Mother knew she was defeated. With Manuel and Paco's planning she had defeated herself, but she would not admit defeat. "Pay the Spanish Government this fee," she told Manuel. "If it is to the Spanish Army or to America . . ." her voice faltered, but she was too proud to cry, "then I send him to America."

Father spoke hurriedly, knowing that enough had been said. "Since this is your mother's wish, tomorrow, Manuel, when you send the money to the Spanish Government, write, also, the letter to Pedro saying our Kepa is coming to Idaho, America."

Mother said, "I will be the one who writes the letter to Pedro. I trust he can still read Basque?" Father nodded. "His letter to me was written in Basque."

"Good." Mother smiled bravely at her dear ones around the table. "Why put off until tomorrow what can be done today? I will write the letter now. Carmen, bring me the pen and the paper for the writing of letters. María, stop your tears and

22

wash your face. What has happened is finished. We must send our Kepa to America with joy in his heart. . . ."

Again Pedro's voice brought the boy back to reality. Again he asked, but this time gently, "What happened, Godson? Can you tell me?" Kepa struggled to find a right reply. "Mother changed her mind. I think Paco and Manuel helped her change it. They told me what to do and I did it. Perhaps María helped most of all. The Little Mother said I was to come. She said she was sending me." Kepa smiled at his godfather. "Anyway, Godfather, I am here where I want to be."

Gently Pedro laid his hand on the boy's shoulder. "You are here where I want you to be," he told him. To himself, he thought, The boy is shy. He feels strange with me. I must not push him. Someday he will tell me.

5 PEDRO GOT OUT OF THE CAR, motioning for Kepa to follow. "This is where you buy your herder out-fit, young Kepa."

The boy looked at him in surprise. "I have my clothes in my portmanteau," he said.

"You'll need other things," Pedro answered, "than what are in your portmanteau."

"I have little money." Kepa was embarrassed.

"It's like this, Kepa. I pay you a monthly wage and found." Pedro laughed. "Found in herder language means food. You keep the cost of what other things I buy for you in a little book. At lambing season next year I pay you what you have earned in wages. You pay me what your little book says you owe me for the things I have bought for you." This was reasonable, Kepa agreed.

They bought boots, blue jeans, and a sweater. Pedro looked at the boy's beret and decided against substituting a hat for it. That would come later, he thought. They also bought envelopes and writing paper, a pencil, and the little book for the accounts. "This about does it as far as clothing goes," Pedro said. "You can keep the clothes you brought in your portmanteau at my

24

house in Boise for when you go back in a year or two. Right?"

Kepa nodded. "Yes, when I have money enough to pay for my passage and enough saved to put a new slate roof on my father's house."

"I am your godfather," Pedro said seriously. "You do not owe me for your passage here. Your return ticket back to Spain is another matter. You may pay for that, but we will cross that bridge when we come to it."

They kept on buying. They bought a bedroll and a tent. "Do you have a knife and a whetstone?"

Kepa was mortified. "A knife, yes, but I forgot the whetstone." Pedro added a whetstone to the pile. They looked at guns. A gun? A gun of his own? The boy could not believe that this miracle could happen.

"Do you know how to shoot?" Pedro asked him.

"I can learn," Kepa said faintly.

"You'll need to learn. You'll need to be a good shot. There will be times when you will need a gun." They bought the gun, a carbine, and ammunition for it. The miracle had happened. Kepa owned a gun. But he was worried. "All these things are costing many pesetas."

Instead of answering the remark, his godfather said, "I am going to put you with Tío Marco for this first year. He is old and cranky but he is the best herder I have ever had—hardly ever loses a lamb. He is a good shot, can hit a dime for a target. He will teach you all there is to know about sheep and shooting and also how to figure not in Spanish pesetas, but in American dollars and cents."

Their purchases made, the man and boy rode toward the ranch in silence, each lost in his own thoughts. The car bumped over the ruts in the road; even though there were still patches of snow along the way, the road was dry and dusty. Kepa looked at the land, flat, sand-colored, covered sparsely with clumps of grasslike plants and low bushes, gray-green in color, blending in with the yellow-brown sand. There were no real trees, no thick wild grass, no rivers in sight. In the far distance were foothills covered with stunted, twisted trees and behind them high, blue mountains tipped with snow. The hills and the mountains framed the brown, bare, desolate world under a deep-blue cloudless sky. Kepa looked at his godfather but he could find no words to express his awe at a world so bare and big and endless.

Suddenly the boy broke the silence. "What about a dog? Does a shepherd here in America have a dog?"

"Oh, yes," Pedro answered. "A herder would be lost without his dog. Chris raises sheep dogs and gives them to some of the herders, although not to all of them. She is particular about where she places a dog for training."

Kepa did not know what to say. He was too proud to ask his godfather if he thought his daughter might give him a dog, but Pedro answered his unspoken question. "She left Tío Marco a young dog a few months ago. He has his own dog, an old one he has had for years. Chris felt that the old man and the old dog could train a new one splendidly. If the new dog takes to you, I imagine she will give it to you since you, also, will be trained by Tío Marco."

Kepa was relieved. He was certain the new dog would take to him, and he might let it wear Tinka's collar. He asked, "Is it a great Pyrenees mountain dog like we have at home? You re-member Tinka." At the name Tinka the boy's voice had sof-tened, Pedro noticed. He remembered his own homesick days when he had come to America. How long ago that was, and the scar it left was his memory.

"No," he answered Kepa's question. "We do not use the great Pyrenees mountain dog for sheep in America. We have found that the sheep relate better to smaller dogs, and it is the

26

dog the sheep respect and obey, not the herder. The dogs Chris raises are a cross between Australian shepherds and English sheep dogs." He pointed ahead. "Look." He sounded excited. "There is my ranch—the house and the buildings, the sheep and the horses—the result of fifteen years' work, but it has been worth it. I have been lucky."

Kepa saw a small ranch house, a large barn, long sheds, and fenced pastures. "These," Pedro said pointing to the long sheds nearby, "are used for lambing, and those over there are the bunkhouses where the herders sleep when they are here at the ranch."

Kepa gave a small cry of pleasure. "So this is an American sheep ranch! This is where I will be."

His godfather corrected him. "This is the headquarters only. The herders bring the ewes here for lambing in February and keep them here for shearing and until the lambs are strong enough for the trail. You missed this year's lambing which is the high point of the year, but you will get in on the shearing."

At Kepa's confused look, he repeated. "The ranch is head-quarters only. You will range your band across the desert to the ranch, here, for lambing, a distance of about four hundred miles."

"That's a lot of miles to take a flock of sheep, isn't it?" Kepa asked. "It takes that many miles of grazing to feed twenty-five hundred sheep," Pedro answered.

The boy could not believe he had heard correctly. "God-father Pedro, did you say a flock of twenty-five hundred sheep? Twenty-five hundred?"

"I did. Tío Marco's band numbers that many. We say band not flock. Carlos' band is nearly three thousand." Then he added in explanation, "His band is the twin band. Then I have two thousand that I do not have a herder for. The herder I had last year left me to go back to Spain."

Kepa looked at his godfather. He felt dizzy and wondered if his mind or his stomach was spinning. Pedro laughed. "I know how you feel. It was the same for me when I came. America is a big country. Things are done in a big way here."

Godfather stopped the car before the ranch-house door. "We are in time to eat," he said, leading the way into the house. "You remember my wife. She comes out here from our house in Boise, almost every day during lambing season and shearing time." Kepa did not remember her too well, but he did not say so.

The man and the boy went into the kitchen first, a clean, bare place looking more like a hospital room, Kepa thought, than the kitchen where a family spent most of its time. One entire end of the room was filled with the biggest stove Kepa had ever seen, and along the sides of the room were sinks and work-tables. It looked like a place to work quietly, quickly and not a place where laughter and songs were almost a part of the smell and taste of cooking food. Rosa, the cook, a young Basque woman, turned from the stove to greet Kepa. "This does not look much like your mother's kitchen in Spain, does it?" she said smiling at him. Kepa shook his head. A vivid picture of his mother's kitchen flashed before his eyes. Instead of a stove there was a fireplace with a crane and blackened pots hanging over the coals and a hearth with two long benches, where the family sat during the storms of winter keeping warm and cozy and, as they said, "toasting our toes."

Near the ceiling, on the walls of his mother's kitchen were strips of white cotton cloth embroidered in red yarn. The walls were bright with hanging copper skillets and pans and shelves of copper bowls and kettles. On the table, covered with a red-checkered cloth, were great brass candlesticks holding squat, fat, homemade candles. Huge hams wrapped in white cloth and strings of pearl-colored garlic and onions and green and scarlet peppers hung from the rafters.

28

"I know what you're thinking," Rosa told him. "Sometimes I think that way too, but this kitchen is built to get the biggest amount of work done in the smallest amount of time. Big and quick, that's America," she said. Kepa, laughing, followed his godfather into an even larger room.

The room they entered was a long one, its only furnishings a long table, benches, and at one end a large heating stove. Seated at the table were about thirty men, all Basque, mostly young men in their twenties, a few older men, and Tío Marco, the oldest, the best herder, the best shot, the best sheep-dog trainer, and the crankiest. Tío Marco knew what was said of him and believed that he held all the titles honestly and was in no mind to relinquish any of them.

Since he was to be put with Tío Marco for his time of train-ing, Kepa looked at the old man with special interest. The boy had hoped the herder would look like the old shepherd of the Pyrenees, and in a way he did. They were both Basque, erect, strong, proud men. Work had gnarled their hands, and time had whitened their hair. They both were old, but in their gathering of years, their harvest had been different. The old shepherd was serene, quiet, secure. He wore his years as a king wears his crown, a mark of royalty. Tío Marco's years had hardened him. He did not have the peace of quiet, but rather the heartbreak of silence. Tío Marco carried his years as a burden and although he carried them with pride, he was conscious of their heaviness.

The other men at the table were not all herders; some were horse wranglers, taking care of the pack mules, the teams, and the saddle horses; others were the ram master, the camp tender, and the extra hands hired to help out during lambing and shear-ing time. There were two women, Godfather's wife, and Rosa, who was the camp cook and also the camp tender's wife.

Kepa wondered if he would ever know all of them by name and what their work was. He had never heard of a ram master or a camp tender. He was confused by so many new people, but, also, he was hungry. The huge platters and bowls piled with mountains of food set in double rows down the long, oilcloth-covered table looked wonderful. The men gave most of their attention to eating, but there was some talk. All of them spoke Basque; nothing was said in English. As the boy ate and listened he felt better and better.

After the noon meal, the men went back to the shearing chutes and pens. One of the men walked with Kepa. "You are Luisa's younger brother," and added, "My brother married Luisa, your sister." Kepa nodded. He thought he had recognized the young man in the dining room.

"So you are Juan," he said. "Your brother said to tell you that he missed you."

"I miss him too," Juan answered. "I almost went home several weeks ago when I got my wages after lambing season. I had saved enough money and I wanted to go back, at least for a visit. You know how it is, I was so homesick for the Pyrenees and so glad that I would soon be there." Juan stopped talking. He seemed embarrassed. Finally, he began again. "To make a long story short, when I got paid I celebrated. I gave a kind of going-away party every night, and before I knew how it happened I had spent all my money. I did not have enough left to go to Spain. Now I will need to work and save for another year, and I am more homesick than ever." Then he added as if in excuse, "This happens to many of us. We save all year and in a week—poof—it is gone."

Kepa thought, This won't happen to me. I will work and save and go home when I have enough. To Juan he said, "We'll be seeing each other often and we can talk about home." Juan looked at him, but did not answer as he went away to help separate the bleating ewes from their baaing lambs.

30

6 THE SHEARING CHUTES AND PENS were behind the lambing sheds. The pens were filled with milling, frightened ewes bleating in panic because they were separated from their lambs. By the pens were the chutes, which were movable fences making an alleyway where the shearers with hand clippers stationed themselves.

In the background, half encircling the chutes, were about a dozen camp wagons, once brightly painted in many colors but now faded and old, dust-covered and travel-worn.

"They belong to the shearing crew," Alberto, the camp tender said, pausing by Kepa's side as Juan left him. "They are the best crew in the country. Mexican, I think they are. They bring their families with them up from Mexico and travel from ranch to ranch at shearing time. Keep mostly to themselves."

Afternoon shearing had begun. Herders and their dogs drove the ewes into the chutes. As a ewe passed a shearer, he grabbed it by its hind legs and at the same instant began using his hand clippers to clip its wool. The men were fast workers, shearing by hand as many as a hundred and fifty sheep a day. They had to be fast. They could not afford a wasted movement. As the sheep kept coming, the men kept grabbing and shearing. They were paid by the number of sheep they sheared, and shearing-season wages had to last their families for a year. Besides, bets were made on which man could shear the greatest number of sheep, so it was pride as well that speeded their shearing.

Shearing camp was a noisy place of many sounds: the bleating sheep and the lambs crying for their mothers, the barking dogs carrying out the calling and whistling signals of their herders, the teamsters shouting orders, the wives of the shearers cheering their men and urging them to clip faster, the excitement of the betters when a favorite won or fell short of his goal, the chatter of the shearers' children playing and squabbling by their camp-wagon homes. Each sound was distinct and separate, yet blended together into a noisy but not unpleasant din.

Shearing camp was a busy place. As a ewe was sheared it was branded by a man who dipped a branding iron in dye and slapped it on to the sheep. This did not hurt the animal, but added to its feeling of indignity.

Tally men counted the sheared ewes by tens and drove them into pens where eventually through the patience of the herders and the intelligence of their dogs, each sheared and frightened ewe found its wooly and frightened lamb.

As the fleece fell from the ewe, a man gathered it into a neat bundle, which weighed about ten pounds. These bundles were carried to the weighing platform and put into a long sack. A man stood at the bottom of the sack tramping the wool with his feet to pack it down tightly. When a sack was filled, the opening was sewn together; then it was weighed. "Each sack should weigh about three hundred pounds," the foreman, who had been explaining what each man was doing, told Kepa.

The weighed bags were loaded into huge freight wagons drawn by mule teams to the railroad in Boise to be shipped to market. When one wagon was filled another took its place, and the first one started on its long haul into town.

Kepa realized that despite the noise, activity, and seeming confusion, there really was order, efficiency, and planning. Each man knew what he was supposed to do and did it quickly and expertly. Kepa thought of what his godfather had said, "America is a big place. Things here are done in a big way."

He asked the foreman, "When do I start to work?"

"Tomorrow," the man said. "Notice when a black sheep is sheared, its fleece is set to one side so as not to mix it with the white? Your job will be to gather the black fleece into bundles."

"There won't be many bundles," Kepa said, disappointed that he might not work as hard as the others.

"There will be plenty." The foreman laughed. "There is always one black sheep to every hundred."

Shearing time lasted several weeks. It was a happy and busy time for Kepa, and he liked being a part of all of it. He liked the feeling of being among men, and although he was the youngest and the newest member, he felt he was accepted and was treated as an equal. The men remembered their own first year of herding, and although they never talked about it, each man knew how much the year had cost him. Each man knew, looking at Kepa, how dearly the boy would pay for his year of experience. Their acceptance of him was their way of giving him their understanding and fellowship.

Between the end of the day's work and the evening meal the men enjoyed challenging one another to contests of strength and skill. At first, Kepa was too shy to participate, but he watched intently. He always had taken part at home, but with boys his own age. The men, noticing the boy's interest, began to urge him to join in the fun. "Get in here, boy, and try," they shouted. "Show us what you brought to America from our Basque country, Spain. Teach us what we have forgotten since coming to America."

Then Alberto offered to bet that Kepa could beat Carlos in weight lifting, although Carlos, one of the herders, was both older and larger. The men began betting for and against him, and Kepa, spurred on by the excitement, did as the men suggested, "Get in there and try." He was no match for Carlos and lost. At once Carlos challenged him in the wood-chopping match. Ever since Kepa had been old enough to lift an axe, he had chopped his share of the winter wood supply at home, so he accepted Carlos' challenge with enthusiasm. The cheering was loud and the betting heavy but the contest ended in a draw. Kepa was excited. His blood ran hot in his veins. His muscles flexed and tightened. He felt alive, eager, confident, a young man among young men. He was the challenger now, taking on Carlos in the high kick as well as in the high leap, and won both matches with honor.

Alberto pretended to be annoyed that Kepa had not won every match. "I was the first to bet on you," he grumbled, "and you made me lose a day's wage."

"Wait until next year and bet a month's wage on me and win," Kepa retorted.

"I'll remember to do that," Alberto answered.

Kepa felt pleased with himself. He had not done too badly in the contests, and he had joked man-to-man with Alberto. At home he had been thought of as the little boy who listened to other people's jokes. Today he felt ten feet tall!

After the evening meal came party time. Kepa helped the other men carry the tables and benches out of the long ranch house to make room for the dancing place. "There will be plenty of girls to dance with," Carlos told him.

"Girls?" Kepa asked in unbelief. "Girls? Where will they come from?"

"Boise," Carlos answered. "Boys and girls from Boise and their parents come out to sing and dance with us. Don Pedro's daughter, Chris, will come, I think. She always does." Kepa's new-found confidence melted. Girls, he thought in dismay. Not my sisters or my cousins or my aunts, but strange girls that I have never seen before, excepting María Cristina. I guess I know her—a little.

Later he watched María Cristina whom everybody called Chris, but he watched her from a distance. At last he had to admit that she was the prettiest, the best dancer, and the most popular of all the pretty Basque girls there, even though she was so very American. Every time she came near she smiled at him, but she did not speak until the night before the last one of the shearing-time fiesta. "Why don't you dance with me?" she teased as she danced past the door where he stood with Juan.

"I do not dance American dances," he answered stiffly.

"I do," Juan said taking Chris from her partner and whirling her out on the dance floor.

Homesick, Kepa thought disgustedly. Why doesn't he go back to the Basque country if he is so homesick instead of staying here dancing American dances?

Later in the evening, Chris and her father found Kepa still standing by the door watching the dancers. "Chris reminds me that you had a guitar with you the day we met you at the railroad station," his godfather told him.

"Yes, my sister María gave it to me. It belonged to your brother Diego."

Pedro's eyes lightened in pleasure. "Diego's guitar? That boy was born with a song on his lips. Do you know any of Diego's songs?"

"Yes," Kepa answered. "He taught them to me." Then he added shyly, "That's how I made friends with the Americans in the railway car coming to Boise. I sang them Diego's songs."

"Good," his godfather told him. "Do you have it with you?"

"It's in the bunkhouse," Kepa replied.

"Get it. Chris and I will wait for you here."

Before he knew how it happened, Kepa was singing Diego's songs. At first, everyone sang with him, but after a while they fell silent, listening to the young boy sing of his Pyrenees mountains and valleys, another world away.

At last he finished. He had sung all Diego's songs. How proud María would have been, he thought, if she had known that Diego's songs had made Basque hearts happy in Idaho, America. He wished he could tell her but he knew he never would. Things of the heart must be kept decently clothed.

Chris came to say good-night. There were tears in her eyes. "Tomorrow night my Boise friends and I will show you how much we thank you for your songs," she said softly. After she had gone the boy remembered that he had not answered her. He had not said a word, not even good-night.

Long before sunrise the next morning the bunkhouse was alive with noisy activity. There was none of the usual before-breakfast grumbling. Even the sleepyheads were on the move, trudging from bunkhouse to ranch kitchen, misshapen shadows in the gray world of before dawn. Carlos, swinging his lantern and whistling one of Diego's songs, caught up with Kepa. The boy joined his whistling and soon the entire line was whistling a song of the Basque Pyrenees. Rosa opened the ranch-house door and stood in a glow of yellow lamplight laughing and welcoming them in to eat. "It's easy to know that this is the last day of shearing," she called to them, "and that a new herding season begins tomorrow."

"Tomorrow. Tomorrow," the men shouted with joy for the beginning of a new year. But with the joy was mingled a feeling of sadness, for tomorrow each man would go his way alone; the herder with his band of sheep, the wrangler with his mule herd, the extra hands to find another job on another ranch. Only the Mexican shearing crew would leave together, their families and caravan taking to the open road. No herder knew what the year might have in store for him. He knew only that whatever it was, he would have to face it alone.

"Hot cakes," Carlos shouted. "Ham and eggs," another man added, and other herders joined with "For a breakfast like this we could stay here forever. Rosa, you are a jewel."

"What happens tomorrow?" Kepa asked.

"We take to the trail," Juan answered. Then Carlos explained, "The lambs are now strong enough to follow their mothers over the trail. Tomorrow we start!"

Kepa had another question. "Do the sheep and the lambs, the mules and the dogs and the herders start at the same time?"

Alberto laughed. "You are as full of questions as you should be of pancakes. No, not all at the same time. Each herder takes his band, his mule, and his dog. The first band ready is the first on the trail."

"And the first band on the trail gets the best grass and water holes," Carlos added, finishing his breakfast and heading for the door. Soon the long room was empty, each herder impatient to get the day's work over and be first on the trail at tomorrow's dawn.

By suppertime, shearing had come to an end and everyone was ready for the evening's fun. It was then that Kepa had time to remember Chris's telling him that she and her friends would do something to show their enjoyment of Diego's songs. In worried embarrassment the boy decided he would stay in the bunkhouse and not go near the party.

After awhile, Juan came looking for him, saying, "You're late. Get moving. The party's starting." Not knowing how to refuse, Kepa went with him.

When he entered the ranch house it was almost as if he were

back in the Basque country at a village fair. The girls and boys of Boise were in Basque native dress dancing joyously and perfectly the old-time Basque dances. Their joy was contagious, spreading to the herders as group after group took the center of the room to perform a favorite dance.

Soon Kepa found himself one of a group dancing with Chris. Laughingly he told her, "You aren't American at all. You are a beautiful Spanish Basque."

"I'm a French Basque too," she answered. "My mother is French Basque, remember?"

Kepa remembered the old Basque saying, "*Zaspiak-bat.*" He said comfortably, "Seven is one."

"Yes," Chris agreed. "Four Spanish provinces, three French provinces, one Basque people."

*2nd Part*

# TRAILING
# IN

7 THE DAY OF DEPARTURE began early. In the shadowy dawn the ranch house, the bunkhouse, and the commissary were filled with milling men; the horse and sheep corrals with neighing, kicking mules, bleating sheep, and baaing lambs. Barking dogs were everywhere.

Breakfast was a hurried and rather silent meal; each man's thoughts were on things more important than talk or jesting. As each herder finished eating, he took his noonday lunch, which Rosa had put up for him, and went to take his gear to the mule corral for packing. Each action was deliberate, thoughtful. Nothing must be forgotten. Each man, also, was impatiently wanting to be first on the trail.

On his way to the bunkhouse, Tío Marco was stopped by Pedro, who beckoned Kepa to join them. The older herder had not spoken to the boy although Kepa had noticed that often he had been watching him keenly. "This is Kepa, the boy I spoke to you about," Pedro said. "As I told you, I am placing him in your good hands for training."

"Well, I can train a sheep dog, I guess I can train a boy." Tío Marco spoke unhurriedly, giving no indication of pleasure or displeasure. "Although," he continued, "In my day a young herder trained himself." Looking directly at Kepa, he said, "On my first day I was given a dog, a mule, and three thousand sheep and told to take them to summer range and bring them back."

"I know," Pedro spoke quietly. "The same thing happened to me. That's why I want it to be different for young Kepa."

Suddenly Tío Marco clapped Kepa on the shoulder. "The boy and I will get along," he told Pedro. "No?" he asked, looking at Kepa, who nodded. At least Kepa hoped they would. Pedro laughed, leaving them together.

"Come on. I begin the training," the herder said.

The old herder and the new, young one went to the corral to get their mules. Tío Marco was given the same one he had last year. "You two seem to understand each other," the ranch foreman told him, "but the one the boy is getting is young and frisky. Stubborn, too, and mean." The man looked at Kepa as if wondering if the boy could handle a stubborn mule. Apparently he decided that the boy could, saying, "Better show him quick which one is master before the brute gets the notion he is boss."

"I will," Kepa answered, again hoping that was the way it would be.

Tío Marco supervised Kepa's packing; the wooden pack-saddle first, and on it the folded tent, the bedroll, his roll of clothing. Then the food—"grub," they called it, from the commissary. Two men were there, checking and double-checking the list as they handed out the supplies: bacon, flour, rice, beans, sugar, dried fruit, coffee, and cans of milk and tomatoes. Grub to last at least five days until Alberto, the camp tender, came with more. After the first visit Alberto would come only twice a month with a string of pack mules loaded with provisions.

Again Tío Marco supervised Kepa's packing half the grub supply, and added a plate, bowl, spoon, coffee pot, and fry pan. "My mule will carry the Dutch oven, the kettle, lantern, canteens, and ammunition, along with the rest of my load. We understand each other, my mule and I." Tío Marco put Kepa's carbine in its scabbard and tied it on to the boy's packsaddle, not trusting it to his inexperienced hands. "Where it will be safe and handy," he explained. On top he tied the guitar, wrapped for protection in a cloth. The old man was painstaking about load balance, the knots, and the give to the ropes holding the pack. He is a good teacher, Kepa thought. After today I will know how to pack my own mule.

While Tío Marco packed his own mule, Kepa had a word with his. "I'm calling you Patto-Kak," he told the skittish animal. "Not because you remind me of the Patto-Kak, ponies of the Pyrenees, but to remind myself that I, being Basque, am more stubborn than you are." The mule rolled his eyes wickedly, trying to rid himself of the wooden packsaddle and the heavy pack.

Tío Marco, leading his mule, and Kepa with the newly christened Patto-Kak on a tight lead, went into the yard where the sheep dogs were waiting, tense and eager, for the first sight of their masters and the signal to go. Tío Marco's signal was so quick Kepa did not see it. The dogs did and rushed to his side.

The two dogs looked very much alike. They were small, black and white, with tan trim, their outer coats stiff and coarse, but Kepa, remembering Tinka, knew their inner coats were soft and thick to insulate them from heat or cold. Their tails were bobbed. "Cut short to keep the burrs from getting in them," Tío Marco explained.

The younger dog had one dark eye and one light one. Although as alert as the older dog, he seemed quieter and not as confident. "Timid," the camp tender said, looking at the dog critically.

"Not timid at all," Tío Marco answered testily. "Hasn't found himself yet."

Alberto understood. A dog under Tío Marco's training was not to be doubted by a camp tender or anyone. "A good dog, though," he said hastily.

The sheep had wakened at the first ray of sunrise and now were moving under the flockmaster's tally out of their corrals. For each twenty-five ewes, a bellwether, a leader sheep, was put in the moving line and a black sheep for every hundred. There were twenty-five hundred sheep in Tío Marco's band. Carlos had the twin band of three thousand, and the third one was about the size of Tío Marco's. Juan called to Kepa, "I'm to have the third band. Pedro gave me back my job as herder. I have my own dog and my own mule that I had last year. I'm the lucky one." He seemed to have forgotten that he had been home-sick. Perhaps he really doesn't want to go home, Kepa thought.

Tío Marco's band was the first to leave on the trail. As usual, at the beginning, there was noise and confusion, the tinkle of the bellwether's bells adding to the din. But once set on the trail there was silence. The dogs, ever watchful of a straying sheep or a lagging lamb, ran before, beside, behind the browsing band, nipping a leg where necessary. The sheep feared and respected them.

The pack mules, resigned to their loads, followed the sheep, now that they were on the trail not needing to be led. The herders, each with his staff, followed behind the sheep, the dogs, and the mules. They were in command. The dogs and the mules knew this, but the sheep obeyed only the dogs.

The ground, the patches of shrub and rocks, the sky, the sheep, and the trail of dust they left behind them were one color—earth color—with no contrasting hue to sharpen or re-lieve the drabness. Slowly the sun moved across the sky; slowly the day moved across the eternity of time. Slowly the sheep moved across the desert, and the dust trail flattened itself over the land. The silence was oppressive, as heavy and as suffocating as the dust. Occasionally, it was broken by the tinkle of the bellwether's bell or the shouted command of the old herder to his dogs, but instantly it closed in again, choking sound into stillness. Kepa wished that Tío Marco would talk or sing—anything to break the unreality of the silent world. He looked at the old herder and wondered how many years and miles he had walked this trail in silence, having no one to talk to. But he has me now, the boy thought and wondered if the old one were lost in his own thoughts, if the habit of silence had imprisoned him or if there was nothing he wanted to say. The boy remembered the old shepherd of the Basque country. How different he was from this old herder of America. The old shepherd had accepted time; the old herder had taught himself to endure it.

8 MIDDAY CAME. The sheep stopped grazing to rest in the small shade of shrub and sagebrush, each ewe sheltering with her body her own small lamb from the sun's hot rays. The pack mules drowsed. The old dog curled up by his master. The young one lay alone. "Don't hurry him," the old herder said. Kepa was surprised. He had thought the old man had been napping.

They ate the lunch Rosa had packed for them. Tío Marco began to talk. "The sheep will rest until late afternoon. Then they will graze until sunset, and at sunset we will make overnight camp."

A question had been bothering Kepa. "How do you count them?"

The old herder explained patiently what he thought the boy should know. "You mark the count by the bellwethers and the black sheep. They keep their places in the moving band. In a few days all the ewes also will have decided their own places in the band. There will be the leaders, the followers, and the tailers. Even though they scatter for a time they will find their own places again. You soon will learn where each belongs and will be able to tell if some are not in their usual places."

Kepa looked at the resting sheep. They looked alike to him. How could he ever learn to know which ones were not in their right places? Then he remembered his small flock at home in the Pyrenees. He had known each one of them very well. "Twenty-five hundred is a lot of sheep," he said. The old herder did not answer. His gaze was on the distant hills. The boy sensed that conversation for now was ended.

In late afternoon the sheep roused and began to graze again, the dogs urging them on, slowly. By sunset they had reached night camp. Kepa could see that the place had been used as a campsite before, perhaps many times before. There was a bed of dry brush on the ground, stakes for a tent, rocks making a campfire place for cooking. How did the herder know, he wondered, that the sheep would reach this camp by sunset? He looked around for a spring or stream or water hole. "No water here," Tío Marco said, sensing the boy's unspoken question. "The sheep will get the water they need from the dew on the plants they eat in the early morning. If there is dew they do not need water every day."

The sheep had bedded down for the night. The man and the boy took off the packs from the mules and tethered the animals out to graze. Tío Marco showed Kepa how to cut sagebrush for under his bedroll. "Pine needles are better," he said. "In the high country you will cut pine boughs and place them with the needle branches in and the boughs toward the edges, but here in the desert you use what you can find."

The old herder put up his tent and helped Kepa with his. "You store the food and your clothing and whatever you have inside the tent to keep them dry and safe. If it is not storming you sleep on the ground outside, with your carbine always handy."

The old man cleared most of the ashes from the rock-rimmed fireplace, made a fire, and cooked their dinner. He was as de-

liberate and thorough with these tasks as he had been in loading
the pack mules. When dinner was cooked the old man fed his
dog first, giving him bits of food by hand, but when Kepa tried
to do the same, the young dog would not accept the food
handed to him. The herder spoke harshly. "Put the food on
the ground near him. He will eat only out of his master's hands.
Don't push him, boy." Then he said more kindly, "A herder
learns to take his steps one at a time so he may never need re-
trace them."

They ate their meal in silence, cleaned their dishes, and put
them away in their tents. Dusk had come to the night camp; the
shadows had lengthened; the sheep were still. The old man
lighted the lantern and stirred the fire coals. "Get your guitar,
boy, and sing to the stars. It helps." Then as if he spoke only
to himself, he added, "I had a harmonica once, but I lost it
somewhere along the trail and. . . ." He sat looking at the
smoldering campfire. "And with it, I guess, I lost my songs."

Singing, Kepa found out, did not help. It made loneliness a
sharper pain, bringing home closer and yet keeping it farther
away. In memory the boy saw again his father's *caserío*, the
big ancient house cupped in a valley of the Pyrenees, sur-
rounded by its fields, its pasture, its vineyard, and the encircling forest. He went again through the wide Dutch door
to the ground floor of the house where the cow and the donkey,
the sheep and the pigs, each in its pen, were housed. The
animals were put out to graze as soon as the sun had washed
the land of the penetrating cold of night. When the shadows
lengthened they were brought back inside the walls of the old
house and bedded down for the hours of cold and darkness,
warm and safe, a part of the family unit.

In memory the boy climbed the wide stone steps leading to
his mother's bright, friendly kitchen, but even in thought he
dared not stop there for he knew that he would see his father

and Little Mother, his sisters, and probably José, his godfather's brother. He dared not stop to picture them, nor to pat Tinka, asleep on the mat by the door.

Quickly the boy's mind pictured the granary, the room at the top of the house, where corn and wheat were stored for the animals and vegetables and fruit were dried for family use, but even this did not help. The remembered sights and sounds and smells of home smothered him, choked him with unshed tears. No, he thought sadly, singing brings memories and memories bring no comfort. Aloud he said, "I do not know how to sing to the stars. I can sing only to what's in my heart."

Kepa put the guitar in his tent. The old herder was asleep, wrapped in his bedroll, his old dog asleep beside him. The boy looked over at the young dog asleep by the fire. "Tinka," he whispered, but the name did not fit. The boy unrolled his blankets and crawled in between them, but he could not sleep. He could not push from his mind the thoughts of home. He thought of the last time he had seen Tinka, and the last talk he had had with his father.

Now he was not in his bedroll under the stars in a strange world called America. He was home again in a Pyrenees valley, ready to set forth to an unknown land across the ocean, but still at home among the things he knew and loved. His beret sat at a rakish angle on his thick black hair. His *charmarra* was buttoned and his *bota* tied to his belt. Strings of *chorizos* like necklaces of spicy smelling flowers were around his neck. His guitar was slung by its leather thong over his shoulder, and in his hand he carried his *makela*, his staff, the symbol of the shepherd, the master of his flock. He was on his way to Idaho, America.

The boy and his family, a line of ten, went single file down the wide stone steps, through the wide Dutch doors, past the dooryard, where Tinka was asleep on the door mat and the little donkey was patiently waiting for the portmanteau and the sack full of food to be tied on his rounded, fat sides, one weight balancing the other.

"But where is Tinka's sled?" Kepa asked in surprise. "Tinka likes better than anything to haul my sled through the snow or my cart, if it's summertime." Kepa looked at his father question-ingly. "My dog has always taken my things to the village."

Father motioned for the others to start down the mountain trail. He put his hand on his youngest son's shoulder, but he did not look at him. There was a moment of silence. At last Father spoke, "Tinka cannot make the journey down the moun-tain and back up again, my son. He is too tired from a lifetime of service and too old from a lifetime of years. He has earned his rest. Do not grieve that today he sleeps and cannot go with you."

Again Father was silent, thinking of the words he must choose for this last talk with his young son, this boy beginning his manhood journey into the years. Abruptly, he said, "Today you come to the first fork in your trail. Remember, my son, al-though *you* travel a new trail, the old one is still there for the people who walk it. Little by little it changes, old people die, new ones are born, things happen or do not happen. The people walking the trail do not notice the changes, but you will notice them when you return. When you leave this trail today it will never be the same for you when you return to it."

The man again stopped talking and again began anew. "What I am trying to say, Kepa, is that once you leave home you have, in a way, left it forever. Two things will hurt you when you come back. One is that living has not stopped just because you have gone. It has taken place as it always has, only you have not been a part of it. The other thing is that what was real yes-terday may not exist tomorrow. Let that knowledge, my son, steel your heart against hurt when you return to us." Kepa hoped he understood. He was not certain.

Father stopped to unbuckle the wide leather spike-studded collar from around Tinka's great neck, wakening the dog from his sleep. "Take this, young Kepa, to remember your love for your first dog and to help you share that love with your new one in America." Kepa took the collar and, blinded by tears, stooped to pat his dog good-bye.

"Do it quickly," Father urged. "Pat him once and go on. It would only disturb him if you communicate your grief. Learn now and never forget it—if you must grieve, keep it locked within you. Do not show it. This is the Basque way."

Kepa moved, turned, sat up, still wrapped in his blankets. Stars shone down on a sleeping world. The campfire glowed. This was not the Pyrenees. This was America. He had wanted to come and now he was here. The boy lay again on the hard ground beneath his blanket. Finally sleep came to bring him comfort.

9 MORNING SUN ROSE over the flattened land, tinting the earth and sky with the same bands of color. The sheep moved and began to graze. The lambs romped and played, flaunting their friskiness. Tío Marco and his dog, Kepa and the young dog following, climbed a small rise of desert sand to look down on the sheep. If they were quiet, calm and feeding, all was well.

The days moved along slowly; only the bad ones stood out to be counted. One afternoon wind brought a threat of rain. The sheep, sensitive to every weather change, scattered uphill. It was hours before the dogs and the herders had driven them down to the flat land near camp to bed down for the night. Another night Patto-Kak broke his tether. At dawn Kepa found him and led him back to camp to be loaded with the pack for the day's move to a new site.

The camp tender came with his string of pack mules bringing camp supplies for the herders and salt for the sheep. He brought letters to Kepa from Paco and Manuel, from Mother and Father. They said everything was fine at home. They said they missed him. Somehow the letters made him lonelier than before. Tío Marco said, "Read your letters, boy, and be glad you get them. At first one writes a lot and the answers come pouring back. Then something happens. One stops writing and the folks stop answering. I guess it's difficult to answer letters that have not been written."

After the camp tender had gone, the days seemed more silent than ever. Kepa understood; it was not that Tío Marco did not want to talk but that he had lost the habit of talking. The old herder was a good teacher both for Kepa and the young dog. Kepa watched him give his signals by whistle, by hand, by shouted order. He watched the old dog respond to them and the young dog learn them. The boy learned them too. He also learned how to take care of his gun, how to keep it clean and dry, safe and always near at hand. He learned to shoot. The old herder's praise, "Good shot, boy," was a welcome one. He learned what plants are good for sheep at one season and poison-ous at another. He learned to watch the sheep and know what caused them to act in certain ways at certain times.

The boy learned that sheep scatter uphill when they sense a coming storm, but move downhill when they sense danger from an enemy. When other dangers surround them, they make a circle with their bodies, putting the lambs in the center for safety. In trying to protect them, they smother them if the dogs and the herders do not keep the animals less tightly massed to-gether. When a lamb strays and a ewe cannot find it, she will go back to the last place where it had been with her. When the lamb lags she will walk backward, coaxing it along the trails.

Kepa did not learn these things by being told about them. If the herder had told him, the boy would have listened, would have agreed, and probably would have forgotten them within a span of days. But now as he experienced them, they were ex-plained to him. He lived them. They became part of him.

Again Alberto came with his string of pack mules. Kepa was surprised to see him; he had not realized the visit was due. He thought, how slowly the days go by, and how fast the weeks. This time Godfather Pedro came with the camp tender. The boy was delighted to see him. He was someone from home. Best of all there was talk, good talk, around the evening cook fire and later by lantern light and starlight.

"Carlos is having trouble with the twin band," Pedro told them and then explained to Kepa, "We put the ewes with twin lambs in one band because it takes them twice as long to get half as far between now and autumn." At Kepa's look of surprise, he said, "A ewe won't feed one lamb alone. Both lambs must be fed at the same time. To get two lambs at the same place at the same time isn't even a miracle. It's an accident." He laughed, but then said seriously, "If I could get another herder I would put him with Carlos to help him, but all the good herd-ers have been hired by this time of the year."

Godfather and Alberto stayed two nights. Before he left, Pedro said, "Chris wants to know how you like the dog." Kepa said, "I like him fine." There was more than liking in the boy's voice. There was longing and hurt. Pedro decided to talk of other things.

When Godfather and the camp tender left the next morning, Kepa missed them. Silence and monotony settled like dust around their campsite and the days followed each other in dreary succession.

Then everything went wrong. Patto-Kak broke tether again and this time went farther before Kepa found him, brought him back, and hobbled him. "You're staying here," Kepa told him, "Remember, I am more stubborn than you."

A ewe lost her lamb and Kepa and the young dog tracked her back to the last campsite, but a coyote had killed the lamb. It was the first one they had lost. Coyote tracks, now that they were in the foothills, were numerous, and Kepa could hear their mocking, nighttime laughter in the surrounding hills.

There was not the rain there should have been for this time of year. Day after day hot winds blew across the land. The last water hole had been dry, and for days the sheep had not had water. If there had been dew on the shrubs and plants, the sheep could have gone waterless at least for a week, but there was no dew. The wind had dried everything in its sweep across the land.

Now that they had reached the hilly country of stunted juniper trees, the rock patches were more frequent, the shrubs farther apart, and each hour of travel became more difficult and slower. A half day's distance away, the old herder knew there was a large spring at the mouth of a stream. The dogs were urging the sheep band toward it. Twice the sheep had stampeded, trying to return to their last watering place. Tío Marco was impatient. "Stupid beasts," he grumbled, "If one sheep stampedes, every sheep in the band will stampede, and if one falls into a canyon, all of them will try to fall into the canyon."

Kepa agreed with him. He remembered the old shepherd at home telling him, "Sheep have a group mind. No matter how large the flock, they think as one sheep." Kepa grinned, thinking of his flock of twenty sheep in the valley of the Pyrenees. Still, he thought, he had learned a lot from that small flock that was being put into use now.

Besides being impatient, Tío Marco was worried and uneasy. His unease communicated itself to the dogs and through them to the sheep. Kepa followed the herder's gaze. A thin line of dust curled against the distant horizon. "Sheep?" Kepa asked.

"Cattle, I think. We must beat them to the spring. We can make it before sunset if these stupid sheep do not scatter again."

**10** THE NOON SUN BURNED THE LAND and the dry wind stirred the hot air. The sheep rested fitfully. Patto-Kak tried to rid himself of his hobbles. The old dog lay near where the herder sat, but neither was napping. They were watching. The young dog lay by himself, but both he and Kepa, also, watched the sheep and the distant horizon.

A separate dust cloud had detached itself from the long, thin dust line. The man and the boy watched it moving in their direc-tion. Tío Marco said, "We break camp now. By midafternoon when the sheep start to browse again, we will be ready to move them." They began loading the mules. An hour went by. The sheep moved, fanned out, began to graze. The pack mules were ready to go.

One of the last chores Kepa did for each camp move was to put dirt on the cooking-fire ashes to smother any tiny spark the wind might flame. As he was doing this, the expected horseman rode into camp. "He's one of a rustler band. I've had words with this man before," Tío Marco said to Kepa, going forward to meet the stranger. As usual, the old dog, when he was not with the sheep, was at his master's side. They went together— the old herder and the old dog—protecting the rights of the sheep under their care.

At first the rustler shouted in English, and the herder shouted as loudly in Basque. After a few minutes the horseman switched from English to Spanish. "I tell you, don't take your sheep to the spring up yonder, I need it for my cattle."

Tío Marco now also spoke in Spanish. "I need it for my sheep."

"Take your sheep some other place," the man said gruffly.

"That spring is never dry," Tío Marco answered reasonably. "There will be enough water for my sheep and the cattle you are driving." Kepa noticed that the old herder did not say, "your cattle."

Apparently the man had noticed it, too, which added to his rage. He said furiously, "My cattle won't drink after your sheep have muddied the water."

Now Tío Marco was angry. "My sheep muddy the water? Bah! It's the cattle that walk in the water and dirty it." The old herder turned his back on the horseman and gave the signal for the dogs to start moving the sheep.

Whirling his horse, the rustler rode back the way he had come, shouting, "I warned you!"

Tío Marco turned to look at him, also shouting, "My sheep need water. I take them to water!"

The dogs had trouble herding the sheep toward the spring. Time after time the band turned backward on the trail instead of forward as the dogs were urging. "I should think they would smell the water and travel toward it," Kepa said.

The herder answered impatiently, "They do smell water. That's why the stupid animals want to go back to where they remember they had it."

It was nearly sundown before they reached the spring, had driven the thirsty animals to the water's edge to drink, and later had seen them bedded down for the night. The old man said, "We won't put up the tents tonight. Tomorrow morning as soon as the sheep have been to water again, we will move on.

It's only a two-day drive to the next water. They can make it."
Then he added, looking back at the dust cloud on the distant
skyline, "I want no trouble with that man. He's a bad one."

"Will he steal the sheep?"

"A lamb or two, maybe for their own meat supply, no more.
Who could make a fast getaway with slow-moving sheep?"

At dusk the wind increased its flurry. "Blowing up a storm,"
the herder said. Rain clouds blotted out the moon and the stars.
The dogs and the herders stood guard as they always did when
the night was black. At dawn, the clouds hid the sunrise, but
the sheep moved, went down to the edge of the spring and began
to drink again. "The rustlers are on the move, too," Tío Marco
said, looking at the nearing darker line against the banking rain
clouds. "But we will be gone before they get here. They can
have all the water they need."

Most of the band had finished drinking and were browsing on
the grassy bank. Breakfast had been eaten; the cooking fire
smothered; the cooking utensils cleaned and packed. Kepa took
Patto-Kak's hobbles off and tethered the mule with a shortened
rope. "When are you going to learn who is boss?" he asked,
slapping the mule playfully as he prepared to put the pack
saddle on. The mule flattened its ears and bared its teeth, but
made no move to bite or kick. "I think we are beginning to
understand each other," Kepa said, laughing.

The two herders packed steadily but unhurriedly. There
would be plenty of time to get their band away from the spring
before the rustlers and their stolen cattle would arrive. But the
men came sooner than Tío Marco had thought. Less than three
hours after sunrise, they rode into sheep camp, three men driving about fifty longhorn steers. Yesterday's visitor was in the
lead. He had a gun in his hand. Tío Marco faced him, the old
dog at his side. "Now that you are here, you can stay here,"
the rustler shouted. "A sheep band can't move without its

dog." Raising his gun he took aim. There was a shot and a whimper of pain.

Kepa could not speak, could not move. He saw his own gun, where he had hung it on a branch of a juniper tree, but he could not reach out for it. The boy could only look in frozen horror at the old herder bending over his dog. Then, realizing the dog was dead, he shouted in anger, "Why didn't you get me instead of my dog? You cowards—to shoot a dog!"

The men and the steers thundered by. Instantly the sheep began to bunch, putting their lambs for protection into the center of their circling bodies. In a flash the young dog jumped among the flock, nipping the frightened sheep, driving them backward, giving the lambs room to breathe. Kepa went with the dog, pushing and shouting. The dog and the boy worked together, instinctively, neither one needing to give nor to have a signal.

It was long after midday before the sheep were calm and resting. Kepa went to find Tío Marco. The old man sat hunched by the fresh mound of earth where his dog lay buried. He needs hot food before we begin the new drive, the boy thought, unpacking the coffee pot, the frying pan, the tin of coffee, bacon and bread, and making a new campfire. When the food was ready he tried to lead the old herder to the campfire to eat, but the man refused to go. He kept saying, "Why did he do it? There was water for all of us." Tío has to eat, Kepa thought. Food will give him strength to walk away from what happened here. The boy brought the food to the old one, coaxing him, but again the herder refused it. Again he said, "Why did he do it? That dog was all I had."

The clouds, threatening since dawn, now opened and rain poured down. The sheep sought shelter in the sage. The boy was worried. He did not know which to do—give the signal, when the rain stopped, for the dog to start the sheep moving and perhaps from habit the old man would follow, or stay at this camp for another night. Alberto was due late today or sometime tomorrow, but he would think that the band would be a day or two farther along the trail. Since his schedule was to leave supplies first at Carlos' camp, then at Marco's, and at Juan's last, he would not come along this trail and would have no way of knowing that Marco's band was not where it was supposed to be. If they stayed here it would mean the camp tender and his string of mules would have to backtrack, which would cause delay. Kepa's grub supply was getting very low.

The rain stopped as abruptly as it had begun. The sheep moved out from the sheltering sage and began to browse. There was water and there were enough grass clumps and shrubs to feed on for awhile longer. The boy looked at Tío Marco. The old one was in no condition to travel. Kepa made his decision. They would stay where they were. Tío Marco might feel better after a night's sleep. Tomorrow's food would be tomorrow's problem.

The boy unpacked Tío Marco's mule and his own Patto-Kak and hobbled them. He put up Tío Marco's tent, but he left his own folded. Quicker packing for morning, he thought. He put the uneaten food on the ground for the young dog. "Eat it," he said gently. "As for me, I'm not hungry."

It was dusk now. He lighted the lantern and again went to where the old herder sat unmoving, uncaring. "Come to bed, Tío. Your bedroll is waiting beside the campfire."

The old man shook his head. "He slept beside me every night. Tonight it will be the same."

"That's fine, Tío. I'll bring your bedroll here." When Kepa brought the bedroll and stretched it out on the ground, Tío Marco said, "Good. Now I can sleep beside my dog."

Kepa made a last circle around the band. The young dog walked beside him. The sheep were sleeping. The boy went again to the new made mound. The old herder was asleep in his bedroll beside it. Kepa raked the campfire so the coals would smolder and die, put out the lantern flame, and crawled into his own bedroll, exhausted, worried, and heavy-hearted.

The water in the spring lay clear and deep. The night wind whispered in the sagebrush and the chaparral. The young dog lay in the shadows. The young boy slept by the smoldering camp-fire. Moonlight bathed the rain-wet land, making it almost as light as day. The old man mumbled in his sleep. The night passed slowly, slowly giving way to the gray light of dawn.

Kepa wakened, startled, frightened, sitting upright, looking around him. His first thought was for the sheep, but they were quiet. Nothing disturbed them. He looked toward the place where the herder was sleeping. All was quiet there. The boy pushed himself back into his bedroll. Perhaps a dream had wakened him. Then he felt something against his body. He looked and at first could not believe what he saw. The young dog lay curled at his side. Kepa put his hand down gropingly, not daring to believe what he wanted to believe. His fingers, then his hand touched the young dog's head. The dog did not move but lay relaxed as if at last he had found where he belonged.

Kepa began to cry. As long as he could remember he had never really cried. He had not known what crying was, but now sobs choked him, caught in his throat, tore at his chest, making his body a holding place of his pain. At length his sobs quieted; his tears stopped. The boy crawled from his bedroll and stood in the moonlight looking down at his dog. "I'm a man now for sure," he told his new friend, "because I wasn't ashamed to cry." He felt empty, but better, stronger, with certainty that he could face the new day that dawn would bring.

**11** SUNRISE IN ITS BRIGHT-TINTED GARMENTS lay upon the horizon, clothing the sky and the land alike in a blaze of color. Kepa and his dog walked to the top of a small sand hill, where they could look down on the band. The sheep were moving, wakened by the first hint of day.

The dog and the boy went back to the campsite. "Why did you suddenly decide to be my dog?" Kepa asked, then answered his own question. "I think I know. I think somehow you knew that now the responsibility for the sheep was yours," and he added proudly, "and mine."

Tío Marco had coffee and fried bread ready for the morning meal. Kepa quietly offered his first bit of bread to his dog. This was what all herders did, and it was what he had been longing to do. The dog took the bread from his master's hand, and now Kepa knew beyond all doubt that this was his dog for as long as they both would live.

Tío Marco looked as he always did, deliberate and steady, but when he began to talk, Kepa could not follow him at first. The old man had gone back in his thoughts to the fishing village of his boyhood in the land of the Spanish Basque. The solitary days, the lonely nights, the empty years of herding sheep in the American West had ceased to exist for him.

"You know my village," he told Kepa, "in the Bay of Biscay, the old fishing village with the wall around it and the watch-tower where day and night the watchman stands to spot the whale? Remember, when he spots it, he lights a fire on the sea-wall. I can hear the drums as they begin to pound and the fisher-men take out to sea." Kepa had seen but did not know the village. He was a Basque of the Pyrenees and not a Basque fisherman on the Bay of Biscay, but he nodded that he understood and the old man talked on and on.

Since Kepa had known him, Tío Marco had kept his talk bone bare, saying only what must be said, using only enough words to make his meaning clear. But now, talk that had been dammed up inside him for more years than Kepa was old, broke through the wall that time had built and flowed out uncon-trolled, unstopping, as a cloudburst pouring its rain on a parched, dry land.

A horseman approached at full gallop. It was Godfather Pedro who had been riding since dawn. Kepa went to meet him, his dog at his side. "Are you all right?" Pedro asked, dis-mounting and throwing the horse's reins on the ground—"ty-ing it to the ground," he called it—to keep the animal from straying. Without waiting for an answer, he continued, "Word came at headquarters there was a rustler gang heading this way, so I left immediately. Carlos had a bad time. They took his pack mule and all his camp supplies and grub. Did they come near here?"

"They shot Tío's dog," Kepa answered.

Without a word Pedro walked to the campfire and accepted the coffee the old herder handed him. "Our whaling ships went as far as Newfoundland," Tío said to him. "Our fishermen saw America before Columbus saw it." Pedro nodded as if it were natural for a sheepherder to sit at a campfire and talk of whaling ships of centuries ago. "My grandfather was a whaler," Tío remarked. "Think I'll try my hand at it."

"Fine," Pedro answered. "Why don't you go back to your fishing village? You've talked of going for years."

"Maybe next year," the old herder said, "when I get enough money."

"You have enough money now," Pedro told him. "I've been banking it for you for years, waiting for you to make up your mind to go. You can go back to your home village and buy a dozen fishing boats."

"Maybe I will," Tío Marco said. "Maybe I'll do that."

"That's settled then," Pedro said quickly, then spoke aside to Kepa. "I hate to do this to you, son, but Tío has finished his days as a herder. He deserves a rest. Is it too much to ask of you?"

"My dog and I can do it," Kepa answered proudly.

Pedro looked at the dog. "I see your dog has found himself, and I have found the young man son I need." Kepa did not answer. He could not trust himself to speak.

"We'll go now," Pedro continued, "before Tío changes his mind. I'll ride his mule and he can have my horse. Put his things in his tent for Alberto to pick up when he comes."

"Will they be safe? When will he come?"

"Safe enough," Pedro answered. "Alberto is looking for you now and probably will meet up with you tomorrow."

"The sheep will have eaten the ground bare by tomorrow," Kepa said. He did not mention that he and his dog would be without food also.

"Start moving them as soon as we leave," Pedro directed, "There is a good campsite a half day from here."

Godfather Pedro put his hand on Kepa's shoulder. "Neither you nor your dog know the trail, which will make the going harder. Look. See the tip of Big Smoky jutting into the sky? Head for it. Keep heading for it. Move the band at a slow and steady pace. Remember what Tío Marco has taught you." Kepa nodded. His godfather's hand on his shoulder seemed to give him the courage he needed.

Tío Marco was still talking. His last words to Kepa were, "Remember, boy, it was not Magellan who circumnavigated the globe. When Magellan died it was a seaman from my village, Juan Sebastian del Cano, who became leader and completed the voyage. Will you remember that?" Kepa nodded as he helped Pedro get the old man ready to start the homeward trail. By early afternoon they were on their way. Pedro called over his shoulder, "Chris will be happy about the young dog finding himself and his master."

Kepa watched them as long as he could see them. Then he turned to his packing, first signaling his dog to gather the sheep for the trail.

*3rd Part*

# THE
# ROLLING
# HILLS

**12** THE SHEEP BROWSED ALONG, slowly, steadily, the young dog nipping the laggers. Kepa walked among them, worriedly, ever on the lookout for a straying lamb, a rattlesnake under a jutting rock or clump of grass, an unexpected deep ravine or dry arroyo where, if a leader went over the steep embankment, the others heedlessly would follow, ending up at the bottom in a pile of injured or smothered sheep.

In the distance, a bed of lupine caught his attention. Tío had told him that lupine in summer was poisonous to sheep although good grazing at other seasons. Was it summer now, the boy wondered, trying to name the month by counting backward to the time he had arrived at the ranch. He thought he had come in March and that they had begun herding in April. Or was it May? It was difficult to name the month or even the season when there was such a dreadful sameness to the days and the landscape.

Tío had said that by June they should reach the foothills of Big Smoky Mountains. "Is this foothill country?" he asked himself. The ground was gradually rising and much rockier than it had been, the junipers grew closer together, the nights were cooler. But was it summer? Would the lupine be poisonous to the sheep? He could not be certain. Finally he decided to take no chances and at a whistled signal, the young dog skillfully veered the sheep away from the patch of lupine toward the opposite skyline.

The afternoon hours dragged by, slow, hot, and still, without the smallest whisper of wind to stir the dust-heavy air and with no sounds except the tinkle of the sheep bells and the baaing of the lambs, punctuated by the bleating of an anxious ewe. As far as the boy could see, nothing moved across the land but his sheep, his pack mule, and his dog. The boy was tired, hot, thirsty, hungry, and the responsibility for twenty-five hundred sheep seemed a greater load than he could carry. But he trudged on.

At last the sun rested briefly on the far horizon, a red ball of fire in a sky of gold, and all too soon was gone, bringing day to its end. There was no lingering twilight. Dusk swept over the land and the sheep bedded down for the night. Kepa tethered Patto-Kak and anxiously looked around at the place the sun had determined and the sheep had chosen for night camp. Was this the regular camping place? Or had he not come far enough, he wondered.

The boy's concern was brought quickly to an end. Nearby was a bare, cleared spot where many times a tent had been staked. Here were blackened ashes of a long-dead fire and a pile of dried and brittle juniper branches that once had been a herder's bed, proof that he had kept to the trail and herded the sheep at a reasonable pace, as was expected of him. They were here where they should be at the dusk of the day.

Kepa wondered how Tío Marco had learned to estimate how far a band could travel in the hours between sunrise and sundown, resting them at noontime when the sun and the air stood still. In the weeks Tío Marco had been the herdsman and he the learner, almost always by dusk they had reached the site where Tío had camped before. The old one had been a good herder, Kepa thought. What the other herders said of him must be true—he hardly ever lost a lamb, he brought the fattest sheep down from summer range, in spring, whatever the weather, he brought the ewes of his band safely to the lambing sheds at the ranch in time to bear their lambs in comfort and safety.

The boy wondered how many years it had taken the old man to learn the secrets of the trail and the skills of the herder. What was the price he had paid for the knowledge? Kepa knew the answer to his own question. Forty years at least the old one had walked the trails in solitude and in silence. He had lost touch with his family and his childhood home. He had lost the habit of talking with the people around him. The boy remembered the night Tío had told him that somewhere along the trail he had lost his harmonica and with it, his songs. He had lost everything he had. Finally he had lost his dog and his touch with reality.

Kepa sat by the unlighted campfire, looking at nothing. "I can't do it," he cried to the lengthening shadows. "I can't live my life alone. I can't walk the trail alone. I can't eat alone every day nor sleep every night with nothing above me but the stars. I need a house and people in it. I need to love them and for them to love me." His words were lost in the thickening dusk. There was no one to hear them, no one to answer them.

How long he sat there he did not know, but suddenly he was brought back to reality by the soft whining of his dog watching him with loving, worried eyes. Kepa jumped to his feet, ashamed of his moment of despair. "I have you." He tried to speak cheerfully. "We have each other." The young dog wagged his stump of tail in pleasure, not knowing the meaning of the words, but knowing and loving the sound of his master's voice.

As Kepa took off the heavy pack from his mule, Patto-Kak tried to bite him. "I hope you are being playful," the boy told

him, giving his mule an affectionate slap. "You better be playing. Remember, I'm a Basque and more stubborn than you."
Then in surprise at what he had said, Kepa repeated, "I am a
Basque. Basque are stubborn." After a second he added, "I came
to America to herd sheep. I am a shepherd. I have earned my
shepherd's crook and I will earn my reputation as a good herder,
as Tío earned his." Then to comfort himself he said, "But it
must not take as long."

Since the boy was too tired to put up his tent, it did not take
him long to unpack. As for preparing his evening meal, that
took less time than making the fire to cook it. There was only
bread and bacon left—tonight's supper and tomorrow's breakfast. "If the camp tender does not come by midafternoon tomorrow, I will butcher an old ewe and you and I will feast on
mutton," he told his dog, giving him the larger share of the
scanty meal.

The dog pushed against him as they sat by the tiny cook fire
watching night creep across the rocky ground, shrouding the
chaparral and the sagebrush in the gray shadows of evening,
turning the twisted juniper into grotesque, dwarf figures of a
nighttime world.

Both the boy and the dog were hungry, and their hunger
seemed to make longer the hours between supper and time for
sleep.

Remembering that once Tío Marco had told him, "Sing, boy,
it helps," Kepa unwrapped his guitar. Perhaps singing the songs
of home did help, because it brought the ancient *caserío* of the
Basque Pyrenees closer to the campsite in Idaho, America. It
brought memories of Little Mother and their last talk when she
had told him, "I need a son in my house." It brought, also, the
memory of his father's farewell words that once having left
home, one never really could come back to it again. Kepa
thought of José's laughing complaint that he rattled around in

72

a too-empty house. He heard again the longing in Manuel's voice as he talked of his school days in San Sebastian and he remembered that when Padre Paco gave him his portmanteau, he had explained that once it held a young man's dreams. I'm not the only one who gets a bit lonely now and then, the boy thought. Maybe that's what growing up amounts to. You are supposed to carry your load alone.

Kepa put the guitar away, and he and the dog circled the sleeping campsite. The sheep were quiet. Patto-Kak was not happily but securely tethered. "You have your troubles too," Kepa told him. The mule flattened his ears and rolled his eyes, but he did not try to bite the boy who had said he was the master. "In the far distant future you and I might be friends," the boy said, but not really believing it would come true. He unrolled his blanket on top of the juniper-bough bed. Tío Marco slept here about this time last year, he thought, feeling comforted, and reached down to pat the dog curled up beside him. At his touch the young dog relaxed and sighed contentedly. "You need me as much as I need you," Kepa said in surprise. "I did not know this before." He kept his hand on the young dog's head. "But now that I know, I won't forget. One of these days we will find you a name." He thought of Tinka and how he had planned to give his new dog in America the same name to keep alive the memory of the old dog of his Pyrenees home. "Tinka does not fit you. You have your own place in my heart, and you must have your own name," he said sleepily. It was his last thought before sleep claimed him.

The night and the camp were strangely still. Even the eerie laughter of the lurking coyote did not completely shatter the night's deep silence.

At the first streak of dawn in the eastern sky the camp came to life. The sheep moved from their night bed-ground. The dog was waiting for his master's signal to go on their sunrise inspection of the animals under their care. Kepa rolled out of his blanket, rubbing his sleep-heavy eyes, and gave the expected order. "All right, young fellow, you seem to be more awake than I am, but we will start the day together." As they circled the band, the boy had his first feeling of pride in his new responsibility. These are my sheep, he thought. I am their herder. I am the one who is responsible for getting them back to Godfather's ranch. He stooped down to pet his dog. "We have a big job to do, but we can do it." The dog bounded away to nip at the leg of a lagging ewe, then came back again as if saying, "I'm doing my part."

All was well with the band. Nothing had disturbed their night or had brought unease to their morning. The lambs frolicked, heedless of the mother ewes' fretful bleatings. Patto-Kak nickered for attention. The bellwether's bells tinkled, making the melody of morning sounds complete.

Kepa started the cook fire with a handful of dead juniper twigs, fried the remaining thick slices of bacon and, with the bread that was left, was able to give his dog a fair-sized meal. For himself, he was content with a bowl of bitter coffee sweetened with the last of the sugar. As he sipped the black, sweet drink, he told his dog cheerfully, "The next meal we have I'll eat twice as much as you do to make up for giving you my share this morning."

Even without breakfast, he decided, early morning was a more cheerful time than dusk. Midday was difficult, also, when the sheep rested and the sun left no shadow and the world stood still.

Kepa led Patto-Kak to the spring for his morning drink. The dog did not go with them, which surprised the boy, because for the last few days the small dog had been his constant companion. Then he heard him yipping, a frantic, warning kind of bark, not at all like the sounds he made when he was herding the sheep, informing his master that someone was coming, or holding his own in the kennel back at the ranch. Kepa never had heard the dog bark like this before. It was a warning of danger.

The boy hurried back to camp, tethering his mule instead of hobbling him because tethering was quicker. The dog was where Kepa had seen him last, near the cook fire at the end of the juniper-bough bed. "What's the matter, fellow? Are you sick? Are you hurt?" he asked in alarm, bending over the dog. The animal did not glance at him, but continued his excited yipping, looking intently at the far side of the bed. Kepa looked, also, and saw with horror a large rattlesnake, coiled, its forked tongue darting in and out of its raised, small, flat head, ready to strike whatever came near.

Kepa's gun was at the side of his bed near the campfire, where he kept it at night, ready, if need be, for instant use. He knew he could reach it in safety because the height of the bed made a barrier between himself and the coiled snake and also because Tío Marco had told him that a rattler cannot strike its own length. His reasoning was quick, but his movement was even quicker. Grabbing his gun, he jumped backward, pushing the dog aside, almost with one motion of his entire body. The gun was loaded! This knowledge brought a flash of thankfulness to the memory of Tío Marco, who had trained him to use a gun. The boy's hand was steady. He felt neither fear nor excitement. Cocking the gun, he took careful aim and fired at the darting head above the coiled rope of body.

When he looked again, he had a moment of exultation, knowing that his shot had hit its mark. "Tío, if you were here you would be proud of me," he said softly. "I wish you knew that I can do exactly what you told me to do." Then he felt ill and sat down weakly, pulling his little four-footed guardian between his knees and looking into his bright, intelligent, worried eyes. "If you had not warned me, when I went to take my blanket from the bed I would have stepped on it. We both know what would have happened then," he said shakily. Then looking over at the snake he exclaimed, "The first rattler I've ever seen! The first shot I've ever had at anything more alive than a tin-can target!" He took a step toward the snake, but could not make himself go nearer to its still writhing body. "When you're good and dead, I'll measure you and count your rattles."

The dog barked again, but this time he was telling Kepa that someone was coming. There was no one in sight and at first the boy could hear nothing. Then came the sounds of hooves clink-ing against the small, sharp rocks that covered the ground. It was Alberto, the camp tender, bringing his string of pack mules loaded with supplies.

For a second the boy felt dizzy, realizing how very hungry he was. But by the time the man and the mules came in sight, he was calmly ejecting the empty shell from the barrel of his gun and putting a replacement in the magazine so that, again, he would be ready for any emergency he would need to face.

Alberto was cross. He had not heard about the rustlers nor what had happened at Carlos' camp nor at Tío Marco's. Because of his heavily loaded pack mules, he had taken the regular trail; whereas Pedro, in his haste to get Marco to the ranch, had taken a shortcut back to headquarters, skirting the trail. Now, even before he dismounted, the camp tender began shouting ques-tions, "Why aren't you where you should be? I bypassed here, thinking you'd be two days farther along. I've been riding the wind out of my horse trying to track you down. Where's Marco?" Dismounting, he threw his horse's reins on the ground, but kept on talking. "Where's the coffee?" he demanded, taking up the pot and shaking it. "This pot is empty. What's for break-fast? What's to eat? I'm as hungry as a bear the first day of spring."

Kepa tried to answer all his questions as briefly as possible,

76

but fully, so the camp tender would know that the circum-
stances, not bad judgment, had delayed the band two days.
When the boy had finished, there was silence. Then Alberto
spoke. "I'd rather that had happened to me than to Old Uncle,"
he said sadly. "He loved that dog. Like he said, that dog was
all he had."

After a few silent moments the man, to hide his emotions,
asked abruptly, "What are you doing with that gun?" Kepa
picked up the empty shell, handed it to him, and nodded toward the dead snake. Alberto turned around to look. "A great
Basin rattlesnake," he exclaimed, surprised. He poked the snake
with the toe of his boot. "What a beauty! Four feet long if he's
an inch." Stooping to look at it more carefully, he said, "Ten
rattles. Cut them off and keep them. I've got a boxful down at
the ranch."

"Does ten rattles mean the snake was ten years old?" Kepa
asked.

"At least ten. A snake grows a new rattle every year, but
from time to time one gets broken off. This one may have been
older than ten. Judging by his size he was old and mean." Looking closer, Alberto gave a low whistle. "Got him with one shot
right in the head," he said with awe.

"Tío Marco taught me all I know about shooting," Kepa said
quickly, trying to hide his pride.

"He taught me too, when I first came here at about the same
age as you are now," Alberto replied. Then turning directly to
look at the boy, he asked, "What else did Marco teach you
about shooting? If he taught you, as he taught me, he repeated
it day in and day out."

Kepa laughed. "I know what you mean—about not shooting
unless there is no other way of protecting what needs to be
protected."

"Absolutely no other way. Beyond all doubt no other way,"

Alberto emphasized and then asked, "What else did he tell you?"

"If I had to shoot I was to shoot to kill, never to wound. That death is quick, but wounding is torture."

The man and the boy were silent again, thinking of the old herder who believed that shooting was only justified for the protection of a responsibility. "There was water enough for both the cattle and the sheep," Kepa explained. "Cattle will drink after sheep. At home we keep them in the same field. Tío thought the rustler, knowing this was true, would accept it."

"Things like this happen," Alberto said.

The camp tender unsaddled his horse, rubbed him down, and put him to graze. Coming back to unload the mules, he told Kepa, "Tío will be all right once he gets back to where he really belongs. He was too gentle a man for this untamed land. My wife's brother goes back to Spain next month. I think Pedro will send the Old One back with him." Then the man said, more to himself than to Kepa, "He was a good man and a good herder."

"And a good teacher," Kepa said softly.

**13** LATER AFTER THEY HAD UNPACKED and put the supplies away, put out the salt for the sheep, taken the pack mules to water and hobbled them so they could graze, the camp tender elected himself camp cook. "Perhaps you can cook as well as you can shoot, but I doubt it," he joked.

"Tío Marco cooked while I did the chores," Kepa said, and added, "But I'm so hungry I could eat the food raw."

"No need to," the camp cook said. "My wife Rosa sent a big pot of beans already cooked and some fresh bread. I brought eggs, too, this time, and I'm considered tops at making omelet." He was, Kepa decided, as he ate an omelet filled with potatoes and sausage.

"I wish I knew how to cook like this."

"You'll learn," Alberto told him.

The sheep, as usual, browsed after their noon rest, and some of them had found the salt piles. "I'll stay tonight," the man decided, "and go to Juan's camp in the morning. Since Pedro knows the rustlers cleaned Carlos out, I know he has sent him a new outfit, supplies, and another mule. Too bad about Carlos, but better to lose your bedroll and your mule than your dog. Cuts a herder to pieces when he loses his dog."

Both of them were thinking of Tío Marco. The old man and the old dog were with them as vividly as if they were sitting there by the smoking fire. To break the heavy silence the man said, "My wife's brother is going back to the Basque country to marry the sweetheart he left there three, four years ago. Says he's going to stay there, but I doubt it. His girl doesn't want to leave the old country, but as for him, he is made for America. He will come back, I think." Kepa listened, but he remained silent. It was good to hear another person talk. The flow of words filled an emptiness.

Alberto liked to talk and he liked being listened to, so he continued. "There seems to be three kinds of Basque people. One kind comes to America, saves every cent he earns, goes back with money enough to buy a little farm or a fishing boat, and lives about the same as he did before he went away except that he has the luxury of money and memories. One kind stays here, gets himself a wife and a band of sheep, and lives a new life in a new world. Then there's the third kind. He wants to go back to the Basque country, but he doesn't want to leave America. He wants two worlds and ends up with neither. That was the way it was with Tío." The man stopped talking and gazed across the empty land. "The old man always wanted to go back," he mused, "but he never got around to actually going."

"I am going home when I get enough money," Kepa said firmly.

Alberto shrugged. "Well, that's what you want now. At first I wanted to go back, too, until I met Rosa. Then I changed quicker than it takes to tell about it." He laughed, then continued, "After we were married what I wanted most was to stay in America and raise a family of Basque Americans. We are doing it, too, Rosa and I, working hard, but getting along."

The sun drowsed in a soft bed of wooly clouds. Kepa stretched, wondering if they would eat again at sundown. He hoped they would. Alberto was a good cook! At the boy's movement the young dog at his side woke instantly, ready for action if action was asked for.

"What about the dog?" the man asked curiously. "Tío always said, some day he'd find his master. Seems he has."

"It happened suddenly." Kepa felt embarrassed to talk about it; the dog's companionship was so new, so complete, so wonder-ful. "The night after the old dog was killed—well, he just came and made me know he was my dog."

Alberto nodded. "It often happens that way. I had two dogs once. One of them acted like I belonged to him, and the other one never paid me any attention at all. Seemed content to think I wasn't around. Then the top dog was killed and at once the other dog took over as if he had been waiting for the chance."

The young dog settled down again at Kepa's feet. There was no order to be obeyed and since his master was near, he was content to sleep.

Suddenly Alberto got up and went to his saddlebags, saying, "I forgot. I brought you two letters." Kepa was delighted. Mail was infrequent. It had been many weeks since he had received a letter. Now there were two. One was from Little Mother of the home *caserío* and one from Alejandro of California, Amer-ica. He decided to read Alejandro's now. His mother's he would save for the lonesome hour between sunset and bedtime.

Alejandro's letter was short, jumping from here to there as he tried to corral his thoughts. He was living in Sacramento, California, America, he wrote. He liked it. They were paying him American money to learn to fix the automobiles. He had a girl, but she was not a Basque, so he was learning English in order to talk to her. Already he could drive a car, he boasted, but he did not know too much about fixing one. A car had too many parts, but anyway even a broken car that one did not know how to fix was better than a sheep. Kepa laughed, reading the letter aloud.

The camp tender laughed at Kepa's stories and then said,

"I'm hungry again. You water my horse and the mules and I'll cook us something to eat."

"Another omelet?" Kepa asked.

"Can you eat another omelet?"

"I could eat a dozen, the way you make them."

This compliment pleased the new camp cook. "*Como no,* of course, of course, an omelet it shall be."

It was dark before the boy had time to read his mother's letter, holding it close to the sputtering lantern flame. There were two pages, but each page seemed to be a letter in itself. Kepa read the first page first, but it turned out to be the second letter she had written, and it did not make much sense. His mother had written, "Dear Son, Kepa. María is going to, also." Going to do what? Kepa wondered. Then he continued reading. "They have asked us our permission. To José, son of First Neighbor, and on the same day as Carmen's. Everything is a flutter. If you were home my heart would be full of happiness, Your Mother." Kepa read the page twice, but still he could not understand it. Then he turned to the second page, which proved to be the first letter his mother had written.

This one was brief, also, but much more understandable, and it held a world of news. Carmen was going to be married, Mother wrote. Her decision for many weeks had been "one day, yes, and one day, no," but at last she had made up her mind; she would marry the young man. Kepa knew the young man's family, but not the man himself. He was the one who had gone to America and now had returned to marry Carmen. "It is good," his mother wrote. "He is from our valley. Carmen is happier than she has been since we told her she was the one we had chosen to inherit the *caserío.* And since, having been to America, he has money, he can repair the house like Carmen wants it. Also, and this is the best, he will be a great help to your father."

Reading these last lines again, Kepa put the letter away. Carmen's husband would take his place, the boy thought, working with Father. They would do everything together, all day every day. They would share their labor and laughter, working in close companionship side by side. Also, Carmen's young man from America, having money, would put on the new slate roof that Carmen wanted.

Kepa thought of María marrying José. That was good. Gentle María would fill José's house with her sweet and loving presence —never again would he need to complain about having to rattle around in a too-empty house. Destiny was strange, the boy thought. Life played hand-in-hand with death. One giving —one taking. Were there rules that must be followed? Was there a plan that must be carried out? He wondered.

His thoughts went back to Carmen. He had known she was to inherit the *caserío*. He had never questioned his parents' decision. By tradition the parents select the child who would carry on. Tradition was never questioned. But Carmen's husband being a help to Father? Doing the things Kepa had planned to come back to do? This was a new thought, one he was not prepared to cope with. It will never be the same for me again, he thought, remembering his father's words that when you leave home, life goes on there, even if you are not a part of it. He also remembered his father's saying that for a Basque the hurts of the heart are kept hidden in the heart.

The boy looked over at Alberto now rolled in his blanket, sleeping soundly. Speaking softly to his dog, Kepa took the lantern, and boy and dog walked quietly among the sheep, ending another day.

**14** BRIGHT MOONLIGHT rained its yellow glow on the sleeping campsite, the small sheepherder tent, little and lonely-looking in the vastness of the land, the cook fire now but a handful of dead ashes between two flat rocks, the boy in his blanket roll, the dog and the mule, and on the nearby hillside the sleeping sheep. The night was calm; not even a hint of wind rustled the chaparral, not even a whisper of wind crackled the dry branches of the juniper.

Stealthily, quietly, something moved, breaking the night's tranquillity. The dog was the first to sense the threat of danger. Then Patto-Kak, tethered to his stake, nickered to show that he, too, had been alerted. The dog's low growl and the mule's shrill whinny instantly awakened Kepa, and his hand reached for the gun beside his bed. Something told him that the dog's growl was a warning for him, not for the sheep. Nevertheless, jumping to his feet, gun in hand, his first glance was to the hillside, but there was no disturbance, no restlessness, no movement in the band. The sheep were sleeping; no harm had threatened them. His unease somewhat slackened, the boy glanced around the campsite, glad that the moonlight made everything so visible.

Squatting by the ashes of the campfire was a wizened, gnomelike figure, his long matted hair, his long bushy whiskers, his bristling eyebrows, his baggy clothing—everything about him—dust-white in the moonlight. Standing dejectedly beside him was a small dust-colored burro. Kepa's glance took in the burro's wooden packsaddle and its meager load with a pickax tied on top. At once Kepa knew that the bent, shriveled, dust-coated old man was harmless. Tío Marco had told him of the homeless wanderers of the mountains and canyons, who avoided trails and men unless they were desperate from hunger and perhaps, although Tío Marco had not said so, desperate from a need, however brief, for human companionship. Their eternal quest was for the gold that the mountains hid and the canyons sheltered. The foothills of the mountain peaks were dotted with abandoned mine shafts. Some had yielded generously their treasure of gold; others just as generously their disappointment. Kepa remembered Tío Marco saying, "From time to time we change our trails slightly for better grazing or a more certain source of water, but always we keep away from mine shafts. They are breeding places for rattlesnakes, hiding places for rustlers on the run, and deathtraps for straying sheep."

But for prospectors he had a kindly feeling. "They are confused wanderers," he had said. "Harmless, homeless, gentle men forever walking rainbows, seeking pots of gold." Kepa, looking at the tired old man, had a surge of sympathy, dropped his gun, and seated himself on his blanket roll.

The old man began to talk. English, Kepa thought, recognizing a few words. Then realizing he was not being understood, the man switched to German. At least, to Kepa, the guttural words sounded like German. Listening to him for a few minutes, the boy decided to try Spanish. "What are you doing here, my friend, at this strange hour between the night and the morning?" he asked.

"I should have known you would speak Spanish or French.

85

All you sheepherders are Basque," the prospector answered in faultless Spanish. "You're just a boy!" he said in surprise. "Where's Marco? What's a boy like you doing with three thousand sheep? You're alone. I checked on it, not even the camp tender with you. Where's Alberto? Where's Marco?"

Kepa answered part of the questions. "Alberto was here, but he went on to visit the other herders."

The old man impatiently repeated his question, "Where is Marco and his old dog? I looked for them farther up on the trail." Then he added, aggrieved, "Marco's old dog would not have growled at me. He was my friend, he and Marco. Where are they?"

"Tío Marco is at the ranch," Kepa answered, not wanting to talk to a stranger about what had happened to Tío and his dog. The wound made by that happening was still too deep, too raw to be reopened.

"Am I permitted to ask why?" the dust-covered little man asked with dignity.

"What may I do for you, my friend?" Kepa replied cheerfully.

"So that's how it is. Well, for one thing, you can tell that dog of yours to stop sniffing and growling at me. Then you can invite me for breakfast, that is if your grub is holding out."

Kepa laughed to show his dog that all was well. "Stay the day with me, friend. I can't remember how long it has been since the camp tender was here. Probably a week ago. I still have about a week's supply of food. You are welcome to share it."

The moon was shadowed now by the gray cloud of before dawn. In a handful of minutes the eastern sky would flaunt the colors of sunrise and the sheep would begin to move. "Unpack your burro, my friend, and take him to water. I will look at my sheep and then cook us a breakfast." With only a nod, the old man led his burro to one side and began unloading his pack-saddle.

86

Kepa did not want to leave his gun at camp while he and his dog went to inspect the sheep, nor yet to show his guest the discourtesy of mistrust by taking it with him. So he gathered dry twigs for kindling, chopped a few sticks of wood, laid a fire, and did other small chores as an excuse for staying nearby while the stranger unpacked his burro. Secretly the boy watched him. As he had thought, the load was a light one, a thin worn blanket, many little bags, all full, but too small to hold any large amounts of food, a goatskin pelt, a knife, bowl, coffee pot and fry pan, and strangely enough a small but beautifully carved box. Tied to the wooden supports of the packsaddle was a hatchet and spade and a pickax which, like the shepherd's crook, is the prospector's work symbol.

"It's safe to go now," the old man said, putting his pack- saddle and his few possessions under a juniper tree. "I'm taking my burro to the spring. You can leave your gun here. I won't be back much before you are." Kepa did not know what to say. He was embarrassed that the old man had known his reason for staying nearby; also he was amazed and amused at the pros- pector's canniness. In Spanish, he said, "*Como no*," which could mean almost anything—Of course, Why not, So be it. Al- ways a safe expression in a tight situation.

Tío Marco had taught Kepa many things in the few months they had been together, but he had not taught the boy how to cook. If Kepa had been eating by himself this morning, he would have had sausage, potatoes, and canned tomatoes sweetened with sugar. The times he had tried to make coffee had not been successful. The drink had been either brackish brown water or bitter black water. Since he was having company for breakfast, he decided he would try again. He had eaten the bread and cooked beans Rosa had sent him, so today along with the potatoes and sausage he would prepare coffee, fried bread, and beans. Fried bread he knew was made with flour, and beans he knew were boiled. Encouraged by this knowledge, he did his best.

Trying to eat the food set before him, the prospector said, "If you begin moving your sheep within the hour, rest them briefly at noon, by sunset you can reach a campsite I know about."

Kepa was doubtful. "I try to herd them as Tío would, if he were here. Why should I hurry them to this place you know?"

"Because the grass and water there are so plentiful you could stay maybe four, five days instead of the one or two night camps you generally need to make." There was a silence. Kepa did not know what to answer. The prospector said, "It's a hidden valley. Marco was the only herder who knew about it."

"How do you know Tío Marco knew about it?" Kepa asked.

"Because I have camped there with him many times. Some-times I missed him; he had been there, but had moved on."

Kepa was still doubtful. "How do you know he had been there?"

The prospector answered patiently, "I know Marco's camp-ing tricks. He stakes his tent looking southward. His blanket roll faces the place where the sheep bed down. His cook fire is always the same, two flat stones with a low back wall of small rocks to shelter it from the evening wind." Kepa thought back-ward to the many places where he and Tío had camped. The man was right. He did know Tío. He knew him well.

The prospector laughed, a high, shrill cackle. "I'm on my way to a sure find of gold this time," he confided. "This time I know I'll find it, but I'm in no particular hurry. The gold will wait. It's been waiting for me to find it for twenty years. It can wait four, five days more." Again he laughed. Then pushing his plate aside and leaning forward to look intently at Kepa, he said seriously, "Lad, I'll tell you why I want you to do this. This food you cook is terrible. That mess of flour and water you call fry bread isn't fit eating for your dog. Those beans will be rocks in my stomach for days. Even though it's half milk and sugar, your coffee is pure poison. Keep on eating this awful stuff and you'll die. Marco's my friend. These are his sheep you're herding. I want you to live long enough to get them back to Marco's boss, Pedro, the man who owns them."

Kepa wanted to laugh, but he knew the little gnome was right. The food he cooked was terrible. He wondered if the pain he sometimes had in his stomach was caused by lack of food or bad food. He had thought he hurt because he was homesick. Perhaps the cause was hunger.

The old man was still talking. "I want to stay with you three, four days and teach you how to cook. Beans must be soaked in water overnight and boiled over a slow fire for most of a day. Made right, the way I do it, Dutch-oven bread is food for a king. As for coffee, you're the first man I ever knew who could ruin coffee. But, lad, you sure know how to ruin it."

The boy said wistfully, "I could do with a bit of learning. I get real hungry." He hesitated, then added, "My dog's feet are sore. The sharp rocks cut his pads. I hate to keep him running after sheep all day."

"I noticed that," the prospector replied. "Guess Marco must have left before the going got so rocky or he would have showed you what to do." The old man went to his unpacked load, unrolled the goatskin pelt, and from one of his many bags produced thread and a needle. "While you pack, I'll fix your dog's feet so he can travel. He's a mite bit friendlier to me now, since you've decided to accept me. Thing I liked about you right off. You were friendly, but suspicious too, like you should be."

His dog's feet had been Kepa's last argument. He could think of no more reasons for not going. By the time he had packed his mule and the old man's burro, his dog was wearing goatskin boots.

"He will worry and chew them at first," the prospector said, pleased with his handiwork. "But he's a smart dog. Before long he will understand why he is wearing them." Then his bright eyes, half hidden by hair, eyebrows, and whiskers, like twin lamps hidden in a bale of straw, twinkled at Kepa. "Herders take care of their dogs," he said in a singsong voice. "Dogs take care of the sheep. Sheep are the reason for herders' and dogs' existence." Kepa laughed, giving the order to his dog to start the sheep on the trail.

**15** THE DOG NIPPED THE SHEEP. The ewes bleated at their frisky lambs and the bellwethers tinkled their bells. Kepa looked over the band. The leaders were leading. The black sheep were in their places. The middlers were in the middle and the taggers at the tail end. Tío had been right when he had said that Kepa would learn to know his sheep, not as a mess of living wool but as individual animals. The boy wondered how a herder knew this. When had he learned it? What had taught him? He never could answer the questions. They were the mysteries of the sheep trail the herders walked.

The small dog in his goatskin boots ran behind the band, beside it, in front of it, circling it, ever on the alert for his master's signals—an arm gesture, a whistle or a call. Behind the band, but watching over it, walked the bent old man and the straight young man and a donkey and a mule.

The sun warmed the day, a small wind cooled it, and the hills unrolled before them, getting higher and higher as they neared Big Smoky Mountain with its eternal crown of snow.

Shortly before sunset they reached a narrow valley that the rolling hills encircled, protected, and hid from all but the few who knew it. Here in this rocky, hilly land of sage and chaparral, twisted juniper and dwarf cedar was an oasis of sweet thick grass. Tall cottonwood trees marked the course of a mountain stream that bubbled out of a rock-roofed spring, meandered through the grass-covered valley for a mile or more, and suddenly disappeared, going underground, no one knew how deep or far. The valley was cool and green. The small sound of the babbling stream, the sweet smell of rain-wet grass reminded Kepa of the little river that divided his father's *caserío* from that of First Neighbor's and brought a moment of homesick pain.

His thoughts were interrupted by the prospector. "See the holes for the tent stakes and the worn grass patch? See the position of the bough bed? See the walled flat stones for the camp-fire?" The old man was delighted to prove that he had known Marco and his way of camping. Now he came closer to the boy and in a kind of croaking whisper confided that this place was his and Marco's secret. "Heard, haven't you, how Marco's lambs are the fattest ones of all the bands when they are sold a month or two from now? Well, lad, the grass in this place starts fattening them. Every year the three, four days Marco stayed here gave his lambs their start. Up yonder in the forest the grass added to what they had, but it started here. Your lambs are not fat. They've had to walk off what they've eaten, but every day they stay here, you can see them putting on fat." The old man was short of breath by the time he had finished his long talk.

Looking around him, Kepa believed what the man had said. The place was green and beautiful, the grass shin-high, thick and sweet. The boy thought, it's a handful of land scooped up from a Pyrenees valley and dropped by mistake among the rolling hills of Idaho, America.

They stayed four days, and they were the happiest the boy had known since leaving his father's house. The gnomelike, hairy, dust-colored old man was a delightful companion and a good and willing teacher. Under his patient instruction, the beans became edible. The bread was light and crusty. The coffee, although strong, when sweetened with sugar and diluted with canned milk and filled with bite-sized pieces of bread, was a meal in itself, tasty and filling.

No more was the time between supper and bedtime the longest and the loneliest hour in the day. Only when the old man talked of the rich gold mines he had been seeking for twenty years did his mind wander and his words thicken. At other times he was clear-thinking and knowledgeable. He had been in many places in Europe as well as America, had traveled many roads, met many different kinds of people, and had many adventures along the way. He knew Spain and the Basque, he said, "like the palm of my hand." He said the names of the cities, towns, and villages, described all the little bays and inlets protected from the winter storms. He knew of the small fishing boats brightly painted red or blue or green and the sides of the road that were dotted with small Basque houses of red and white brick, each one, like those Kepa had seen on the way to San Sebastian when he had left home, having its ancient coat of arms carved high above the doorway. When the man described the road from San Sebastian to Marco's boyhood village, Kepa realized he himself had traveled that road and gone through the village on his journey from his Pyrenees valley to the harbor of Le Havre.

The boy remembered his last day in his home village, the day he had told his family good-bye. He remembered their journey down the snowy trail of the mountainside. He remembered entering the village and reaching the village church where the town crier was announcing the happenings of the day. It seemed unreal to hear him calling the news that the teacher's brother and the postmaster's son were going to America—today.

The church bells began to ring, and the people who had been

standing in little groups before the door of the church had moved aside to let Kepa and Alejandro be the first to enter. The people looked at the boys curiously as if they had not sung and danced with them the night before. Kepa had had a moment of panic. Already, he thought, I am becoming a stranger. He walked slowly with new dignity into the church.

The men and women followed him, the men going up into the church gallery, the women kneeling on the floor below, as was the custom. This was what they always had done.

When the service was over, Padre Paco blessed the boys and their journey and blessed the people they would leave behind. The church bells rang again to speed their parting.

Mother and her three daughters had been the first to say good-bye. The day was half over and their trail home was steep and long. Carmen and Luisa walked arm in arm. They are alike, Kepa thought in surprise, fierce but loving. María walked on Mother's left, supporting her against her grief at Kepa's going. Kepa walked with them to the end of the village street. Their good-byes were said quickly, simply, but leaving no doubt of their love. The boy watched them start up the mountainside. Even on the narrow trail, María walked closely by Mother's side. My sister María's gentleness hides great strength, Kepa thought, and asked himself, "Why do I see them like new people today when I have been with them all of my life?" He could find no answer.

As the boy stood there watching his mother and his sisters depart, José and Luisa's husband came up to him. They, too, were saying good-bye. "Bring Pedro with you when you come back," José told Kepa. "Tell him the house is much too big for a man alone."

"Look up my brother Juan. Tell him I miss him," Luisa's husband said as the two men leading the fat little donkey left the edge of the village to begin the mountain climb. Kepa walked back to the square before the church. It was time to go.

Manuel and Alejandro's father had loaded the portmanteau, the sacks of food, and one filled with Alejandro's clothing into a mule-drawn two-wheel shay loaned to them for the journey as far as San Sebastian by Old Ramón, the village storekeeper.

Old Ramón would go with them. "It is not that I do not trust you with my mule," he told Father. "My mule would be un-happy knowing a stranger was handling his reins. So you see how it is. I must go with my mule and my shay."

In his youth Old Ramón had gone to California, America, and worked in the goldfields for seven years, saved his money, and returned to his village, a wealthy man by village standards. "Did you like America?" Kepa asked him now.

"I liked America, yes," the man answered.

"Why did you come back?" Alejandro wanted to know.

"Why did I come back?" Ramón repeated, surprised by the question. "I went to earn enough money to come back and live out my days here." Then he added with finality, "This is where I belong." Kepa and Alejandro understood his meaning. He was willing to lend them his mule and his shay, but he had no inten-tion of being questioned along the way.

Alejandro had confided to Kepa, "When I get to America I am going to stay there and learn to be a mechanic who fixes automobiles."

"A mechanic? To fix automobiles?" Kepa could not believe him. "What do you know about automobiles?"

"As much as I know about sheep," Alejandro retorted. Kepa noted that although he boasted, he spoke low enough for the others not to hear him.

Old Ramón climbed into the shay and motioned for Father to get in beside him. Father and the postmaster would take turns riding. Manuel and the boys would walk.

Padre Paco had been the last to tell the boys good-bye. "I

would like to go all the way to Paris with you. I would like to see Paris and my old school again. I would like at least to go as far as San Sebastian, but with the teacher, the postmaster, the storekeeper gone, as well as his mule and his shay, I and the town crier are the only ones left to manage the village," he said jokingly, but Kepa knew that the joking was to hide his sadness.

"I should stay with you to help you manage properly," Kepa joked in reply, proud that his voice did not falter. He was learning to keep the things of the heart hidden within his heart.

Old Ramón clucked to his mule and flapped the reins, which made the animal start, although reluctantly. "I don't think his heart is in this journey," Father suggested. Ramón did not answer.

Soon the cobblestone, tree-shaded village street gave way to a dirt tree-shaded country road. The tree-covered hills and the snow-covered mountains behind them seemed to push against and crowd into the narrow roadway. Here and there in a dip in the hills they could see a whitewashed stone and timber *caserío* standing guard over its cornfields and its flock.

With an effort Kepa brought himself back from the past to reality. The past was over. It was finished, but it had been good to relive the memory. The boy looked at the old prospector, and the wall of silence that he had been building to hide his grief over what had happened to Tío and his dog came toppling down in a pile of broken words. "About Tío and his dog," he said, "I want to tell you if I can." He was silent, then began again, "There was enough water for the cattle as well as the sheep . . . even I knew that. Tío thought the sheep could have the water they needed and be on the trail long before the men got there. They came too early. The sheep were drinking. . . ." Again Kepa stopped talking. Grief flooded his mind and he began to cry.

The old prospector sat quietly, patiently waiting. At last, his tears spent, Kepa began to talk again, ashamed at having cried and yet relieved that the storm inside his heart had burst. "The old dog was with him. You know how Tío's dog was always with him? Well, he, the head man . . . he shot the dog and the dog cried and Tío held him until . . . until he died. . . . I think it was the next day. . . . I don't remember when it was, but Godfather Pedro came and took Tío with him. Godfather will send him back to Spain. Tío's mind had gone back to Spain after his dog died. . . . You know how sometimes you know where you are, but your mind goes back to home and the people you love?"

The prospector nodded. His eyes were blotted with tears. "He loved that dog," the old man said brokenly. "That dog was all he had." Kepa had heard those words before.

After a time the prospector said, "I was certain that some day he would fall under his heavy load of solitude. He had lost the ability to communicate with anyone. Lad, he couldn't even talk to me, his friend."

The fire crackled, filling the soft air of twilight with the heavy scent of burning cedar. For the rest of his life, whenever Kepa smelled cedar smoke he remembered the wizened, dust-colored old man and the campfire at dusk in a hidden valley somewhere among the rolling hills of the New World's western rangeland.

After awhile the old man spoke again, looking into the flames of the fire. "Trouble with Marco was he never left home in the Basque land of Spain. Being able to leave home when the time comes and build a new one for oneself somewhere is part of growing up." Kepa wondered if the old gold seeker had been able to build himself a new home having left the home of his father.

The four days had passed swiftly. At tomorrow's dawn the prospector and his burro would strike out cross-country for the gold mine waiting to be found. Kepa and his dog would point their band toward the mountain forest.

"When is Alberto coming?" the man asked. "Your grub is getting low." Kepa shook his head. "I don't know," he confessed. "I can't keep the days straight. They are so alike that one slips into the next one without my being able to separate them by their names."

"Try notching a stick. Put a new notch on it at the end of each day as it slides into the night," the prospector suggested, rummaging through his many small sacks, looking for his own notched stick. "You think these sacks are all alike, don't you? They're not. To me each sack is as different as the thing it holds. This one here holds gold dust. First gold I ever panned. This one is full of my own handmade medicine, a bit of this and that. Good for a cut, a burn, a sprain, or a stomachache. Rub it where you hurt and you're cured."

The old man touched the beautiful carved box Kepa had noticed, holding it tenderly. "This box is my home. Only one I've had in more years than I can count," he said softly to himself. "It keeps some token of everything I have held dear. Hold it, lad. It isn't everyone I permit to touch it. Look at the carving. I did it. Carving fills a lot of empty hours."

Suddenly, excitedly, he added, "Lad, why don't you try carving? Never know what you can do until you try." Rummaging around the pile of firewood, he finally found a piece he liked. "Look at this bit of cottonwood. What do you see in it?"

Kepa looked at it for a long time. Finally he said, "I think I see a blue jay, flying."

The old man was pleased. "Start whittling, lad, while you still see it. You can catch the shape tonight before the daylight fades. The fine lines can come later."

Kepa liked holding the wood in his hands. His fingers seemed to feel it taking shape, almost taking on a feeling of life. Finding

98

his knife, he began to cut the wood gently, to whittle it delicately. "Why haven't I done this before?" he asked. "I've always whittled a little at home, making whistles—things like that." He worked until it was too dark, even by lantern light, to see what he was cutting.

Afterward, rolled in his blanket under the star-filled sky, his dog curled up against him, he kept thinking of the bit of wood until a sleep cloud blanketed his thoughts and blackened out the stars.

At dawn they watered Patto-Kak and the burro, cooked breakfast, ate, and packed. Kepa tied half the food he had left on the burro's pack saddle. The old prospector, tying his small sacks in place, opened one and took out a nugget. "Pure gold," he said, "payment for the good food I taught you to cook." He held it out to the boy.

Kepa looked at the nugget. It reminded him of his godfather's gold watch, which he had coveted so many years ago, and of his dream to someday, also, own a watch of gold. Finally he shook his head and said sternly, "I cannot take payment for food."

The old man laughed his shrill cackle of mirth. "And I never pay for food either. This nugget isn't worth five cents American money. It's called Fool's Gold. Keep it so you'll know the old saying, 'All that glitters is not gold' is true."

Still laughing, he whacked the small white burro and started on his never-ending trail to find his special pot of gold. Kepa gave the word to his dog and the sheep to go in the opposite direction.

**16** KEPA AND HIS DOG WERE TIRED. For three nights they had had no sleep, having stood guard over the restless sheep. Last night there had been no need to guard them, but the boy had feared a repetition of what had happened on the two preceding nights.

Sitting by the cooling ashes of the breakfast fire, the boy felt discouraged as well as tired. He had lost two fat ewes. He did not look at the pelts he had staked out to dry but instead looked at two sheep tails lying on the flat rocks of the campfire. These he would have to show his godfather as evidence that he, herder in Tío's place, had allowed two sheep to be killed.

Why was it, he wondered, that having company was wonderful when it was happening and so awful when the company had gone? Having the prospector had been fun, but since he had left, everything had gone wrong. Maybe it would not have happened if someone had been there to help him or tell him what to do. As for loneliness, he thought, when there was another person around, it melted into nothingness, but when whoever it was had gone away, the loneliness came back to stalk the daylight hours and haunt the nighttime dreams. The quiet of the empty days pushed against him and the night's deep stillness enveloped him in a blanket of worry, doubt, and despair. There were so many things that bothered him, so many things that worried him.

The boy was worried about the food supply. By the reckoning of the notches in the stick, Alberto would come in two or three days, but according to the amount of food that was left, the pack string with supplies was overdue.

He was worried about the sheep the coyotes had killed. He was furious that he had permitted the sly animals, working as a team, to outwit him and kill the sheep. He had skinned them but wondered if he had skinned them properly. How long would it take the pelts to dry, and could he pack them on his mule before they were thoroughly dried?

The sheep grazed slowly, steadily. The young dog stretched out at Kepa's feet, exhausted from the last night's vigil, guarding them. The boy sighed, looking over the rolling hills. There was good water here, but would grazing hold out for another day? Would there be water at the next campsite? He wished he knew what lay ahead on the trail. Next year he would know it better. Next year? Would he be here in this desolate land next year or back in the valley of the Pyrenees that he knew and loved?

Listlessly he picked up the piece of wood he had been carving, turning it in his hands, examining it critically. The head and the body were good, he decided. He had caught something that made them right, but the wings were wrong. They were not blue jay's wings in flight. He began to whittle.

Suddenly the dog barked, an excited welcome. Kepa stood up, expecting the camp tender and his pack string. He could see them coming over the rise of a hill, but there were two riders. The first rider was leading the pack string, the second, a single pack mule. "Godfather Pedro," the boy called out in delight and, taking a longer look, "María Cristina."

"Chris," the second rider laughingly corrected. "Chris—spelled with an *h* in it."

Kepa was looking at Pedro. "Tío Marco?" he asked, afraid to hear the answer.

"We had a letter from Rosa's brother," Pedro answered. "Marco will live with his widowed sister in their childhood home. He will be happy there." Then he added, "Chris and I have come to celebrate with you José's and María's wedding and Carmen's and her young man's too. As you can see, I have brought the best cook in Idaho to prepare the feast."

"And the prettiest one," Kepa said politely, helping the young girl dismount.

Pedro laughed. "She brought her own pack mule loaded with the things she thinks she needs. Her mother insists she ride sidesaddle as proper for a young lady, and she insists on bring-ing her own private tent. So we always know," he said, winking at Kepa, "that a proper young lady is with us." Chris laughed, but did not contradict her father. Kepa, looking at her, thought in surprise, She almost is a young lady. She is taller and sort of different from when I saw her at the ranch. As for the sidesaddle and her own tent, he approved of them. Girls were supposed to ride sidesaddle and not sleep under the stars.

"Since we were coming," Pedro explained, "we brought your supplies. Alberto has gone on to Carlos' camp and Juan's." The man looked with affection at the boy standing before him. He had loved this boy since the day of his birth. Now he was proud of him. No one knew better than Pedro the loneliness of the first days in the countless miles of rangeland alone with a dog, a mule, and a band of sheep. He said to Kepa, "You and I will put the supplies away while our young lady cook unpacks her own mule."

"First, I must tell you something," Kepa said, the red blood of shame flooding his face. The boy picked up the sheep tails

102

and handed them to his godfather. Pedro took them. "These things happen," he said calmly. "Tell me about it."

"Well . . ." Kepa began, "three nights ago—except that nothing happened last night. But the two nights before that—well, the first night and the second night the same thing happened." He was telling it badly, he knew, because he was ashamed. He tried to speak slower, to be more coherent. "My dog and I heard them—the coyotes—and we rushed in where they were barking." Anger as well as shame made his words stumble. "Those sneaky coyotes were working together. While one was making the hullabaloo to get our attention, the other one sneaked in at the far side of the band and killed a ewe—not a lamb, a ewe. The stupid sheep never made a sound to let us know what was happening."

"They never do," Pedro said, "They bleat their heads off when they can't find their lambs, but when they are in distress they never make a sound. Coyotes are tricky animals. They will trick you every way they can."

"I know that now, but the first night I never guessed what those sneaky coyotes were doing."

"Where was your dog?" Godfather asked.

"He was doing his duty chasing the barking coyotes. They are more afraid of him than of me," the boy answered in defense of his dog. "The second night I knew, but I wasn't quick enough. The second sheep was dead before I figured out where it was happening." The boy was silent, thinking, the price of two fat ewes is more cash money than my father ever has at one time.

Pedro waited, but when the boy did not continue, he asked, "What happened the third night?"

"Nothing."

"They didn't come back for a third killing?" Pedro asked, surprised.

"They couldn't," the boy said. "As soon as it was light, the third morning I tracked them down."

"Did you frighten them away?" Pedro sounded amused.

"No, I shot them. Their pelts are over there with the sheep pelts. I hope I skinned them right."

Godfather Pedro put his hand on the boy's shoulder. "Experience is a good teacher," he said kindly.

"It's an expensive teacher," Kepa said, disgusted. Pedro laughed. "*Como no*," he said. "Learning is expensive, but if it holds, it is worth the price."

Pedro began carrying the supplies into Kepa's tent. "Out of grub," he noted. "You must have been eating up a storm."

"No," the boy said, as he also carried supplies into his tent and sorted the food. "I've had company." Then he told about the prospector's visit.

Pedro was surprised. "I knew Hans looked up Marco from time to time, but he never goes near the other herders." The man looked at the boy. "He actually camped with you for several days? He must have liked you." He seemed pleased that the old prospector must have noted the boy's worth. "People around here call the old man "Hans the Loco," but he is loco only about finding gold. He really is a great scholar. The times I talked with him, I've been impressed. He leaves a kernel of wisdom." Kepa nodded, remembering what the old man had said about being able to leave home and make a new one when the time was right. Pedro asked, "Did he show you his carved box?"

Again Kepa nodded. "He let me hold it."

"That's more than he does for me," Pedro said, laughing. "Although he showed Tío Marco what was in it."

"He did? What was in it?"

"Tío Marco did not talk much about it. Although one time he mumbled something about a picture of a young woman and a small gold wedding ring. He said Hans had told him the picture reminded him of Chris."

"Was it Chris?" Kepa asked. His godfather laughed. "Of course it was not Chris. Chris was little more than a baby when Hans showed Tío the picture." Pedro laughed again. "You know how it is—you are fond of two people, you get to thinking they are alike. Old Hans has always been very fond of Chris."

Chris, having unpacked her mule, now came to the campfire, calling gaily, "My mule needs water. My tent needs to be put up, and I need extra wood for the campfire."

"One thing at a time," her father told her, then said to Kepa, "I'll take the horses and pack mules to water. You go cut some wood for Chris and after that put up her tent."

When Kepa brought the wood, Chris had the campfire blaz-ing and food in the blackened kettles. Kepa would have liked to ask her what was cooking; it smelled wonderful, but he was too shy. Instead, he busied himself around the camp until his godfather returned and Chris called the cowboy chuckwagon call, "Come—and—get—it."

"Chicken and Dutch-oven biscuits," Kepa exclaimed, as they sat down to eat. "I haven't tasted chicken since I left home." As usual he gave the first bites to his dog, looking at Chris as he did so, hoping she did not think him impolite. She said laugh-ingly, "I know. Guests always eat after the dogs have been fed. Herders are like that about their dogs."

"You have a beautiful horse," Kepa remarked, hoping to change the conversation.

"Yes," Chris answered, "we have good horses at the ranch." Then, as if the thought had just come to her, she added, "Be-tween lambing and shearing seasons, the herders have vacation. They stay at the Basque Boarding House in Boise. You will be staying there, too. I'll bring in an extra horse for you and we can go riding."

Her father was annoyed. "What do you mean, 'stay at the Boarding House'? Have you forgotten that Kepa is my godson? He will stay with us, when he is in Boise!"

Kepa, smiling to himself, looked at the girl and at her father, thinking, this is what she wanted him to say. Her father doesn't know it, but I do. She forgets I'm used to girls; I have three sisters. He grinned at Chris, but she pretended not to see him.

"Is there more chicken?" Pedro asked. "Kepa and I are hungry."

"More chicken," his daughter answered.

By the time they had finished eating, it was early afternoon. The sheep were resting, the horses and mules were grazing, and the young dog was asleep by his master's side. "It's a lazy time of day," Chris remarked. "What do you do to help the time go by?"

Kepa was embarrassed, but he felt he had to answer. "Lately I've been trying to carve. The prospector got me started," he said shyly, showing her the almost finished jay. He explained, "There is something the matter with its wings."

Pedro answered, looking at the bit of wood, "The wing overspread is too great and—"

"I think it's beautiful," Chris interrupted her father.

Kepa was pleased. "If I can fix the wings I'll give it to you."

"I like it the way it is." Chris reached for the wooden bird. "Thank you," she said softly. "Your first carving."

My first gift to a girl not my sister, Kepa thought to himself, wondering how it had happened. He said politely, "*De nada,* it is nothing," the Spanish way of saying, "You are welcome."

"You haven't read the letter I brought you," Pedro accused his godson, holding out the letter for Kepa. Kepa was surprised. To forget to read a letter immediately you received it was unheard of. Again, he wondered, What is the matter with me? I was so tired and discouraged before they came, and now I feel rested and happy and then to forget all about a letter! He thought about it, holding it, turning it over. I guess I miss not having people around, he reasoned, to make me act like this when they come.

The letter was from his brother, Manuel, a long and chatty one, telling about the wedding party preparations in the two *caseríos* and ending with, "Thinking of marriage must be con-tagious. I have bought a small house here in the village and have my eye on a pretty girl I hope to marry and have live with me in my new house. You will be with us, Kepa. I have always wanted you to be part of my household as soon as I got one." Kepa finished reading the letter aloud and put it back in its en-velope. For some reason, he did not want to talk about it. Chris and her father, also, were silent.

Chris left them quietly, going into her tent. Finally, Pedro said, "Let's walk."

The dog, the boy, and the man walked among the sheep, now feeding in the coolness of late afternoon. "Your sheep look fine," Pedro said. "Every bit as good as Marco's this time of year. I don't know how you manage to put fat on them before you reach the mountain meadows. Grazing on this side of Big Smoky is no better than what Carlos or Juan has, but look at them! Already they are as fat as butterballs. I can't understand it." Kepa had a small temptation to tell his godfather about Hidden Valley but he brushed it aside. It was Tío's and the prospector's secret, not his to give away.

After the evening meal had been eaten and a cool wind had blown away the day's heavy heat, Pedro put a fresh log on the campfire. The three people sat in the light of its flame, enjoying the pleasure of companionable silence, sweetened from time to time by bits of conversation.

Pedro said, "Chris and I must leave immediately after break-fast tomorrow morning. Chris's mother misses her when she's away, so she puts us on curfew." Kepa could not trust himself to answer. The loneliness of the days ahead closed about him.

Noticing his silence and perhaps understanding what was causing it, the girl said, "I'm so glad the young dog likes you."

"We like each other," Kepa answered, letting his hand rest lightly on the dog's head.

"What do you call him? Does he have a name?" Chris asked.

"Not yet," Kepa confessed. "I can't find one that suits him. I thought of calling him Tinka, but then I decided he should have a name of his own."

Chris said sadly, "I've never named a dog."

"Never named one? You raise dogs. Can't you find a name you like?" Kepa wanted to know.

"Oh, yes," she told him, "I have a very special name. Maybe someday I can use it, but I never name the dogs I give the herders. It is their right to name their dogs. The mother dog I have was named when it was given to me."

Kepa asked softly, almost in a whisper, "Would you like to give that special name you have to my dog?"

The campfire lighted Chris's face, aglow with pleasure. She answered as softly as Kepa had spoken, "Yes. The name is Keeper."

"Keeper?" Kepa repeated, not knowing the meaning of the English word.

"The translation into Spanish would be *guardian*," Chris explained. "But to me it means more than just to guard. It means. . . ." The girl hesitated, trying to put into words all that the name meant to her. "It means loving protection."

Kepa nodded, understanding. "Loving protection . . . my dog for me—me for my dog," Kepa said. Leaning over his dog, he repeated, "Keeper, your name is Keeper." The dog thumped his tail with pleasure at being spoken to.

Kepa looked at the girl sitting by the firelight of his campfire, under the starlight of his night camp. Again he repeated the word, "Keeper."

It was his first word in English, the language of America.

108

# 4th Part

# THE WILDERNESS AREA

**17** SLOWLY THE SHEEP WALKED through the days of summer. Slowly they climbed the rolling foothills, trailed through the rocky canyons, going higher and higher into the mountains, deeper and deeper into the forest, forever following the receding line of melting snow.

Today they had reached their first mountain meadow, like some small stage set for a wilderness drama in a forest theater. It reminded Kepa of an ancient Greek theater that was described and pictured in one of the lesson books he had studied at the village school with Manuel, his teacher-brother.

The stage backdrop was a solid wall of jagged peaks, veiled in clouds and capped with snow high above the timberline, towering above the dark border of trees at its foot. The floor of the stage was a grass-green sea crested with wildflowers; the orchestra a jewel-clear lake mirroring the blue canopy of sky. For lighting, an aspen grove screened the sun, making blotches of sunlight and shadow.

Kepa took the loaded packsaddle from Patto-Kak's back, watered and tethered him out to graze. He pitched his tent, storing in it the bags and tins of food. He cut fresh pine boughs for his bed and gathered dry twigs to kindle his cooking fire.

Propping his back against a tall pine growing beside the lake, the boy waited, half believing that actors would come upon the stage and the play would begin.

Nothing happened. The stage remained empty. He saw no other living thing but the sheep, the mule, and his dog, although he thought he could feel small eyes peering at him to watch his movements, small ears listening for some sound that he might make, small noses pointing windward to catch his scent.

The boy's gaze idly circled the lake. Quite close to where he sat, permitting him to see it plainly, was an odd, bearlike little animal, much smaller than a bear, squatting on its haunches at the edge of the lake. The creature's nose pointed out, his ears pointed up, and the portion of his face around his eyes was very dark as if he were wearing a mask. He had a ringed tail, but the amazing thing about the small animal was the way he used his forefeet. They looked like baby hands, and he was using his fingers as a child might, to feel under the sand edge of the lake, hunting for something. The creature was looking for a frog for his supper. Finding it, and getting ready to eat it, he washed the frog thoroughly in the lake, still not looking at what he was doing.

Kepa laughed and his dog looked up inquiringly, then settled to sleep again. Keeper was tired. At the sound of Kepa's laughter and the dog's slight movement, the bear creature pointed his nose in their direction and caught the strange smells of man and dog. He dropped his supper-frog and lumbered off in an awkward, clumsy manner until he reached the nearest tree, which he climbed quickly, and expertly hid himself in the branches.

The boy laughed again, wondering what the little animal was called. He had not seen one like this before and he would like to carve its likeness, but he was too tired to hunt for a piece of wood or to get his knife from the tent. The day had been exhausting for him—the trees had constantly gotten between him and a lagging ewe or a straying lamb.

The afternoon slipped quickly into evening. In the lengthening shadows, the mountain meadow did not look like a Greek theater of long ago. It looked like what it was, a meadow of grass and wild flowers, rimmed by the trees of the forest, watered by a lake, and cupped by the mountains that protected and held it.

Kepa lighted the fire and cooked his evening meal, but he ate with little appetite. He was tired of beans and sausage and sweetened coffee and thought longingly of the good cheese Carmen and the old shepherd made, the fish and chicken dinners his mother cooked, and the juice of the grape his father tramped each autumn. He was treading, probably now, the juicy purple grapes of his vineyards.

For a breath of time, the boy was back with his father in the valley of the Pyrenees half a world away. Again he saw the vineyard, the cornfield, and the pasture. He saw the narrow little stream that divided the *caseríos* of his father and First Neighbor. The families would be even closer now that María was marrying José, and, also, perhaps broken a little by Carmen's marrying a lad who had gone to America and come home again.

Kepa remembered what his mother had written about Carmen's young man having money to repair the house as Carmen wanted it and that he would be a great help to Kepa's father. Had Little Mother written those lines thoughtlessly, Kepa wondered, not knowing how they might hurt a boy in Idaho, America? At once he answered his own question. Little Mother was not a thoughtless person. She was deliberate in everything she thought and did. Her son knew that she believed if a cut needed stitches in order to close the wound, stitches, no matter how much they hurt, should be used. He knew she must have wanted him to be forewarned of change and to know that perhaps his place in the *caserío* might be a little different. Then thoughts of Manuel brought him comfort. He still had a place in the Basque country. He had a place in his brother Manuel's house.

The moon, a flat, golden disk, shone down on the meadow and the lake, blessing them with light. Kepa cleaned the supper dishes and put them away. He and Keeper went to see if the sheep were where they should be, now that night possessed the meadow. They were quiet. They made no sound. Even the bell-wether bells were stilled in the soft thickness of the night.

If I had someone to talk to, the boy thought desperately, someone who would talk to me. He had not spoken to a person nor heard a word spoken in a dozen days. An hour ago, as he cut the twelfth notch on his stick, he kept thinking, Two more days until Alberto comes—two whole days more. I can't bear it. I have to talk to someone now. But there was no one.

The boy tried talking to his dog. "Good dog. Good Keeper," he said and then stopped. What more was there to say? I'm becoming like Tío, he thought. I have nothing to talk about. Keeper tried to help. He looked lovingly at his master. He wagged his tail to show that he was pleased, if that was what Kepa wanted. It did not help. The boy tried to sing, but his heart was unwilling. Diego's songs brought home too close and at the same time kept it too far away.

Later, in his pine-bough bed, the boy could not sleep. The tall pines, encircling the meadow, seemed to stand brooding guard over the sheep and the shepherd. The wind in the pine tops whispered its murmured monologue that was punctuated from time to time by the soft thud of a falling pinecone. There was the gentle lapping of the lake water against its sand-ledged bank, the stealthy pat-pat of the night animals going about their night-time raids, the sudden plop of something falling heavily into the lake, and the distant yowl of a hunting animal and the sharp cry of pain of its prey. But in the great medley of sounds there was nothing, not even the distant sounds of laughter of the coyotes in the canyons, that was like the human voice. Nothing resembled it. Nothing substituted for it.

Kepa, telling Keeper to stay with the sheep, walked around the lake. The lake and the meadow and the mountain behind it were incredibly beautiful, but the boy felt apart from their beauty. He felt that this was the place of the wild creatures of the wilderness. He did not belong here. He felt small and insignificant, alone and lonely.

At the far end of the lake was a large outcropping of rock. The boy climbed it slowly and carefully. Reaching the top, he sat, his knees under his chin, looking up at the aloof, glacierlike mountain that walled one side of the meadow. Far above the timberline in a recessed cliff in the mountain stood a Rocky Mountain goat bundled against the cold of his glacial world in long-haired coat and leggings. Kepa knew it was a Rocky Mountain goat for he had seen a picture of one tacked on the bunkhouse wall at the ranch. The moonlight was so bright the boy could see the animal's stubby horns, and his whiskers looked both longer and thicker than the prospector's. The goat seemed neither afraid nor disapproving of the strange, huddled creature sitting on the rock top far below.

On a sudden impulse, Kepa stood up, shouting loudly, "Hello-o-o, Rocky Mountain goat," and around him, engulfing him, came the echo, *Rocky Mountain goat—mountain goat—goat.* At first the boy called his greeting in Spanish. Then he called it in French and in Basque, and the echo repeated the words, fainter and fainter. He never knew how long he stood there, yelling in three languages his salutation to the bewhiskered goat standing in dignified contemplation in a niche in the mountain peak.

At last, his voice hoarsening to a husky croak, the boy stopped shouting. He felt very foolish, and also very good. He knew he had not shattered the silence, but at least he had made a stab of sound, piercing the quietness of the wilderness. Returning to camp, Kepa told Keeper cheerfully, "I made the mountain talk back to me." Keeper whined. He had not liked his master shouting to the moon. But Patto-Kak whinnied in derision. Kepa told him, "Remember, mule, I am a Basque. I can make the mountain talk back to me."

Kepa did not realize then that on that certain night in a mountain meadow of the Idaho wilderness he had conquered loneliness. There were many times when he felt alone, when he felt he was without companionship or help, but never again did he feel lonely. That night he learned that being alone means one stands by himself—only that. But being lonely means despair at being alone.

**18** THAT NIGHT THE BOY'S SLEEP WAS SOUND and un-disturbed until at the instant of dawn he was awak-ened by Keeper's pushing against him. Although the dog made no other move than the pressure of his body, Kepa could feel his tense excitement. "Steady, boy," he said softly, looking to-ward the sheeps' bed down. The animals were moving slowly out into the dew-heavy grass. The band moved as a group, not as individual animals. Watching them, Kepa thought, as he often did, how the leader must have been the first to waken and start the outward movement, but he could never find out if this was what actually happened. Always, as he looked at them, they were moving as a unit. Even though he constantly saw evi-dence of group-mindedness and group movement, he could never accept the fact that a band made up of twenty-five hun-dred animals could act as one. Sheep were interesting, he thought, stubborn and temperamental, but interesting.

Kepa looked down at the dog beside him, still pushing against him, still tense with excitement. "Steady, boy," he again spoke softly, placing his arm around the animal. Now he looked where his dog was looking, in the opposite direction from the sheep.

Night mist was rising from the lake, a cloud of gossamer silver, and through its billowing veil the boy saw five does, three with slender, dappled fawns beside them. As the mist rose upward, it massed and thinned, at one moment letting him see the deer as dim, unreal, ghostlike creatures, then suddenly revealing them clearly in the bright blue morning, ethereal creatures of grace and delicacy.

"Stay," Kepa said softly to his dog. "You are a working dog. Your work is sheep, not deer." Under his master's touch, Keeper's body relaxed, but he continued watching, perhaps wishing that his work was deer instead of sheep.

After the deer had their morning drink, they began to graze, unconcerned about the sheep, the dog, or the herder. They seemed unconcerned also about each other as if each doe and her fawn grazed alone. The only communication there seemed to be among them was between the doe and her fawn and that was not by sound but by touch. Kepa and Keeper watched them for a long time, the boy fascinated by their slender graceful beauty.

As the mist rose, Kepa could see the length of the lake. At the far end near the rock where he had sat last night, sharply outlined against the lake and sky, a magnificent stag slipped his muzzle into the lake water and instantly raised his great, antlered head, letting the water trickle down his throat. He drank slowly and was as calmly self-possessed as if all the other occupants of his wilderness world did not exist. When he had quenched his thirst, he went with great dignity into the forest behind him and disappeared.

Kepa rolled out of his canvas-covered bough bed. The cold, sparkling air had a buoyancy that made him feel lightheaded as well as light-hearted. As usual he walked among his sheep and watered his mule. Going for wood for his breakfast fire, he whistled a brief Basque dance tune. Soon he was dancing, leaping his length and kicking much higher than his head. Keeper was delighted and ran around his young master, barking and nipping a heel when it touched the ground. The dance completed, Kepa told his dog, "The sheep are stuffing themselves with tender willow shoots. Patto-Kak is stuffing himself with wild flowers. Alberto, probably, will be here tomorrow with supplies. This morning, my friend, you and I will eat half of everything there is left. This is not wise, you know, for the camp tender may be delayed and you and I might get very hungry before he comes, but wisdom is not for the young to use all the time. This morning we may not be wise, but we will feast."

As Kepa and his dog were eating the promised feast, the bear creature came back to the lake shore and repeated his actions of the evening before, feeling for his breakfast frog, finding it, and thoroughly washing it as he gazed across the lake. This time Kepa did not laugh, and quietly put a restraining hand on Keeper as a command to be quiet. Not making a move himself, the boy watched the little masked animal, trying to memorize his shape, his markings, and his ways of moving. As well as keeping his gun always at hand for the safety of his flock, he decided that from now on he also would keep his knife nearby and a piece of wood.

Finally, Keeper nudged his master for another bite of breakfast. Kepa gave it to him. The bear creature looked at them, not in fear but with annoyance, lumbered awkwardly away, and expertly climbed the nearest tree. Kepa could not see him there, but he could feel the bright little eyes peering down at him.

The boy gave the remaining breakfast food to Keeper, got his knife and some wood and began to carve. Time passed, perhaps an hour or two. Kepa was lost to everything but the piece of wood in his hands. He was excited because he was getting what he wanted. As usual, with his carvings there was an instant when the wood ceased to be just a piece of wood and took on a feeling of life. When this happened the cutting became slower and more painstaking, perhaps a deep cut here or a delicate line some other place. That had been true of the coyote he had spent last week in carving as he camped in the foothills with the sheep. A doe and a fawn he had not attempted. He felt too much a beginner to be able to catch their lightness and delicacy, but if he could watch a stag until he felt he knew it, he thought he might be able to show its majesty and dignity. Someday he might try to carve one—someday.

Kepa's carving and daydreaming were brought to an abrupt end by Keeper's bark and Patto-Kak's neigh. The boy looked up, embarrassed that he had not noticed anyone's coming. Since the man was wearing a green uniform, Kepa thought he must be some kind of officer for the Government of America such as he had seen at Ellis Island. The boy spoke to the stranger politely in Spanish. The man answered in what Kepa thought was English. Kepa tried again, this time speaking French. Then he tried Basque. At each of the boy's attempts the stranger became more irritated and spoke more rapidly and for a longer time in his own language. At last, exasperated, he dismounted, went to his packhorse, untied a spade from his pack, and handed it to the boy with another volley of strange sounds and words. Sitting his horse again, he scowled down at the herder. Then leading his packhorse, he rode back in the direction from which he had come. Kepa was mystified by the gift of the spade. What was he to do with it? He was also in a temper at not being able to understand or be understood.

He put the carving away, now being in no mood to work on it. He cleared the breakfast dishes and put them and the spade in the tent, cut kindling and wood for the cook fire, washed his clothes in the lake, rubbing them with stones to get them clean, and swam across the lake and back. The water was icy cold and he felt exhilarated when he came on shore again.

Later, stretched out in the sun, Kepa felt at peace with his world; his moment of ill temper at the stranger's visit was gone. He was curious about why the man had come and what he had been trying to communicate, but was confident that if he knew what it was, he could handle it. He would ask Alberto when he came tomorrow.

Keeper barked. The boy hoped it was not the stranger coming back again, and his hope was granted. It was the camp tender and with him, leading the pack string, were two other riders. Kepa called to them, "Good morning. I did not expect you until tomorrow."

Alberto dismounted. "It's noon, not morning. Look at the sheep resting. They know the time better than you."

"It's been a busy morning," Kepa said. "I forgot the time."

The two other riders had dismounted and were unloading one of the mules. Although he had not seen the boys for many years, Kepa recognized them. They were Godfather Pedro's twin sons. He tried to remember their names, but couldn't. "Brought them with me," the camp tender said, nodding toward the boys. "Taking them to Carlos and his twin band. Another set of twins can't make it much worse." The twins, coming to meet Kepa, laughed. Their laughter was like their sister Cristina's, Kepa thought.

"We wanted to stay this month with you," one of the twins said.

"But Dad said you were too young," the other one continued.

"To make us mind," the first one finished the sentence. They looked alike; even their mischief-filled eyes were alike, twinkling in saucy merriment, waiting to hear what Kepa would say .

"Tell your Dad," Kepa said levelly, "when you stay with me, you obey me." He added sternly, "You better take my word for that and not try finding out for yourselves." Kepa was bluffing, but it worked as he saw respect take the place of mischievousness in the younger boys' eyes.

"We always obey," they said. "Always."

"They're good boys," the camp tender agreed, "although a bit strenuous."

The twins asked if there was time enough for a swim before they had to go. "A short one," Alberto told them. "Then we'll eat and shove on." Kepa was surprised. The camp tender always had spent at least one night with him when he came with the bi-monthly supplies. "There's a forest fire on the other side of the mountain near the trail Juan is taking," Alberto explained. "I want to leave the boys with Carlos, spend the night there, and go on as quickly as I can. Juan's band might be in trouble. Five years ago the Boss lost a thousand sheep in a forest fire. Wind changed, bringing the fire from a new direction. Didn't have a chance. They were trapped." Kepa had not known that forest fires were common in the thickly wooded mountains in late summer. This would be another hazard, he thought worriedly.

He asked about the stranger. The man, he learned, was a forest ranger, an expert woodsman, that the Government hired to help protect the forests. "There's a forest fire lookout station not far from here," Alberto said, "Foresters are good men to have around. They keep an eye on things."

"The one who came by here this morning left a spade," Kepa said.

"What did he say about the spade?"

"I don't know," Kepa confessed. "I didn't even know what he wanted me to do with the spade."

"He told you to use it in case of fire, didn't he?" Alberto asked.

"I couldn't understand him," Kepa explained. "He thought I was a stupid know-nothing because I couldn't understand his English." Kepa's temper returned. "I thought the same of him. He couldn't understand a word of my three languages, not even Basque."

Alberto laughed, "Well, yes, he knows only English," he

agreed, "but English is the language of America, and you happen to be in America."

Kepa was quiet, thinking of what Alberto had said. Then he came to a decision. For many weeks he had been thinking of buying a Spanish-English dictionary, knowing that if he had one, he could learn at least enough English to understand when someone spoke to him. Now he asked if such a book would cost much money. The boy's question also made the camp tender come to a decision. For some time he had been wanting to tell the boy that he should buy new clothes. "Not too much," he answered Kepa's question about the book. "And while I am buying it, I should buy you some clothes. Your shoes are in tatters. You've grown tremendously these last few months— up, out, and around. Your pants come up to your knees and your shirt sleeves to your elbows. As for buttons—" the man shrugged. "They've popped off long ago under the strain of holding things together."

Kepa looked at his clothes in surprise. What the man said was true. "But I hate to spend the money," he said defensively. "The little book must be full of things I have to pay for."

Alberto was exasperated. "The hardest thing for America to teach a Basque is to spend money." The man laughed. "But once he has learned that he has it to spend. . . . " He threw up his hand, snapping his fingers. "—He spends it. Then it's settled. I get you some clothes big enough for you."

"Yes," Kepa answered, "and the book."

The noon meal was now cooked. Kepa gave the call to "Come —and—get—it," and the boys lost no time in taking their places at the cook fire. Kepa had cooked all the food that remained from last month's grub, but watching the boys make the food disappear, he was not worried. They had brought a new supply. What he did mind though, he told himself ruefully, was the twins eating all the cheese that Cristina had sent as "a small treat" for Keeper and himself. After all, they are my guests, he thought, trying to comfort himself. A host gives generously. A host? He was the host? Then he repeated the thought to himself, I am the host. This is my camp. The thought made him happy. He had not felt this way before. The cheese was a small matter in comparison to his new estate.

Immediately after they ate, the party set off for Carlos' camp. "I'll probably be back in four or five days to check on fires this side of the mountain," Alberto said in farewell.

"Good." Then remembering, Kepa asked, "What do you call a little bear creature that wears a black mask?"

"A raccoon," the camp tender called back. "He wears a mask because he's a thief and will steal anything you have that's fit to eat."

"Raccoon," Kepa repeated. "Raccoon." It was his second English word.

The boy put the supplies away, watered Patto-Kak and brought him back to the campsite. There might be an hour or two of sunshine left, which would give him light enough to carve. If the small masked bandit came back, he could watch him and compare what was real to what he had tried to capture in the block of wood.

The boy sat on the lake shore, his gun and knife and partially carved figure within easy reaching distance, hoping the racoon would come back again for his supper frog. While he waited he looked across the lake. The doe and their fawn had returned and stood in silhouette between the blue of the lake and the green of the pines.

Rain began to fall, making a gray curtain between the boy and the deer, which softened their outlines but did not hide them. "How beautiful they are," he said to his dog sitting beside him.

As he spoke, it happened. A long, lean brown-gray animal

124

leaped down from a tree branch upon the back of the nearest doe, imprisoning her forelegs and sinking his jaws into her slender neck. There was a brief struggle, but the doe had no chance. Instantly the other deer disappeared, taking the now orphan fawn with them. The powerful catlike animal dragged its kill into the underbrush.

The incident seemed to have begun and ended in the same breath. What had been life would not be life again. Kepa felt shaken, nauseated. "This is truly a wilderness," he told his trembling dog, "an untamed, wild world that is as cruel as it is beautiful." The boy felt frightened. He was certain the animals had jumped as much as twenty feet. What would it do with a band of sheep?

He looked again across the lake, but the curtain of rain had thickened. Even the lake could not be seen. The wind changed and with it the rainfall. What had been gentle misty drops now became a downpour, pounding the trees and the meadow. In a second Kepa was wet to the skin. He waited, expecting the downpour to stop as suddenly as it had begun, but it kept on and on and on, a hymn of grief, a dirge, a requiem for a small forest creature, the gentle doe.

**19** AT THE THREAT OF STORM and the first hint of rain, the sheep had scattered uphill, deeper into the forest. Kepa lit the lantern. The night was black velvet, and the faint circle of lantern light was more comfort than aid, but he carried the light anyway. His lantern in one hand, his shepherd's crook in the other, he was armed with the traditional weapons of master of the flock. Shouting incessantly to his dog and working with him, the young shepherd managed to get the band back to the comparative flat land of the meadow.

Again and again a crash of thunder hit the mountain wall and bounded back in echo, echo echoing echo, until the entire meadow became a holding cup of sound. The boy felt the thunder's resounding clap above, around, inside him, pounding his heart and brain.

Lightning zigzagged across the sky, splitting the black heavens and lighting the mountain world in brief, vivid flashes of illumination like some unseen evil spirit playing with a torch of fire.

A tree was struck. Kepa saw the zigzag flash of light leap from the sky to continue its zigzag line down the entire length of a giant pine, its fire turning the branches into fingers of red, orange, and yellow color.

Kepa was frightened. What would he do, he wondered, if the fire would spread from treetop to treetop? He could untie Patto-Kak's leash and let him go free; the mule might make it to safety. But the sheep, although they had freedom had not the wisdom to use it. They would be burned.

The boy, automatically shouting orders to his dog, did not know how long he stood, unable to move, looking at the flaming tree. Perhaps it was only a minute. The lashing rain beat against the tongues of flame in a furious battle of water and fire. If there had been wind to add its strength to that of the fire, the drenching rain would have been to no avail. Fortunately, there was no wind. Gradually the flames died. The tree smoldered, and smoke hung low over the meadows, stinging the boy's eyes and throat.

Near dawn, the storm stopped as if on signal. Stars came out to shine down on a wet world. The sheep huddled in wet misery; the tent sagged under its load of water. Sometime during the night Patto-Kak had broken his tether and had disappeared. The lantern light had burned out; there was no more kerosene. The lightning-struck tree still smoked, but there was neither flame nor spark in its charred trunk.

The boy and his dog still walked among the sheep, Kepa pushing against their crowding with his staff, Keeper nipping their legs to make them move apart so they would not crowd so closely together they would smother in their need for the feel of their own kind.

Gradually the stars faded and the sun shone through the clouds to dry and warm the land. Patto-Kak, Kepa thought sadly, was probably down the mountain slope by now, running free, and maybe frightened, over the rolling hills.

The sheep moved out under the sun's warmth, and the boy lay down by the blackened fire. His clothing was wet. The ground beneath his body was wet. Curled close beside him was

127

his cold, wet dog, but the storm was over. The sheep were safe. The boy and the dog slept soundly.

Kepa was awakened when Keeper licked his face. The sun, noon-high, was directly overhead. The sheep were resting, exhausted from their night of terror. The boy looked around the campsite. Everything was drying out. Several hours of bright sunshine could dry thoroughly all that had been soaked by many hours of drenching rain. He remembered Patto-Kak. What would he do, he wondered, without his pack mule? Looking over at the stake where the animal had been tethered, Kepa saw his mule still trailing the broken rope, grazing innocently among the sheep, but keeping a wary eye on the boy and the dog.

Kepa wanted to laugh. He wanted to boast, saying, "We have come to an understanding, my friend. I am the Boss." But he knew better than to boast, at least not yet. He knew that an unexpected move on his part would send Patto-Kak running and kicking. To get him tied again would be a battle of wits and strength. Kepa was certain his own wits were soggy and although his clothing had dried while he slept, his body was stiff and sore.

Very quietly he stood up, not looking in the mule's direction, walking around as if the mule were not there. Patto-Kak's wicked little eyes watched every move the boy made. In a flash, Kepa turned toward the mule and grabbed the broken tether, bracing himself with all his strength against the squealing, bucking, kicking, biting fury of the mule. "So," Kepa told him, "You are in a rage because you permitted yourself to be caught. You are on a short rope this time, boy, until I have time to mend the broken strap." Kepa pretended to be cross, but he really was pleased that Patto-Kak had come back after his time of freedom. "You are my mule now."

There was much work to be done. The tent had stood up under the weight of water that had collected in its folds, and

128

most of the supplies had remained dry. The ones that were damp had to be dried out with the heat of the campfire, which was still to be made. The ashes between the stones were a soggy mess. The kindling and the wood were wet. The matches were wet. It took an hour of time and seemingly a year of patience before Kepa had coaxed the fire to a cheerful blaze and another hour or two to dry the food, store it, and cook a meal for himself and his dog. "I don't know if this is last night's supper, this morning's breakfast, or the noon meal," he said to Keeper. "But whatever it's called, we eat it. No?" Keeper wagged his tail in agreement.

The sheep had wakened and were moving out to browse. Kepa had one more chore to do before darkness fell. Taking his gun and telling Keeper to watch the sheep, he started for the other side of the lake. An animal that could kill a deer, he thought, could kill a lamb or a ewe. Whatever the cost, the band must be safe.

The trail around the lake was wet and slippery, but it had been washed clean of tracks as had the edge of shore sand. On the far side of the lake, however, there were still evidences of struggle. A patch of grass had been flattened, a fern bed trampled, tree branches broken, showing that something heavy had been dragged into the forest. It was not a straight or a swift path, but meandered, turned, twisted, and backtracked. Kepa slowly and painstakingly followed it.

At times the boy also backtracked on the trail as he returned to look across the lake at his own campsite, to see if his sheep and his mule were safe under Keeper's care. It was almost dusk when his search was rewarded. In a shallow cave under an outcropping of rock he found the remains of a freshly killed doe. He also found tracks with wide flat pads and four wide, short toes. He knew they must be the tracks of the long catlike animal that made the kill.

The boy's gun was ready for instant use. He waited, scanning the inside of the cave. Nothing moved. He took a few cautious steps backward. There were no signs of life or movement. The boy did not know if the animal had eaten what he wanted of the doe and abandoned what was left or if it would come back to feast again.

After awhile Kepa gave up. Apparently the animal had gone. Cautiously, the boy retreated. Nothing moved. Before he reached the lake shore he was confident that the animal had gone, perhaps on another forage.

The boy decided not to take the meandering trail he had followed to the cave but a short cut to the lake shore, and then pick up the well-marked trail around the lake. At first all went well. He had noted the outstanding features in the landscape and knew the direction he wanted to go. But soon he became uneasy. He was not lost and in a few minutes would reach the lake, but with each step his sense of unease deepened. He was certain he was being followed. Without changing his pace, he listened. No twig broke. No branch snapped. No bush was pushed aside. Still listening intently, at last he caught a small sound, a steady, soft, pad-pad somewhere behind him. The boy walked slowly, then quickened his steps; the soft pad-pad continued at its measured pace.

The boy turned, jumping to one side, and faced backward. In the soft green light of the forest he saw the animal he had been hunting, a lean, long gray-brown cat with a small, broad, flat head and short, round ears. Around its mouth was a lighter color than the rest of its body, bordered by a darker line. Looking at the animal's eyes, bright, unblinking yellow-green cat's eyes, sent a chill up the boy's backbone. He raised his gun, aimed, was ready to fire. The animal disappeared, leaving no trace, simply merging into the dark green of the forest. Slowly the boy realized he had not killed the animal, not even shot at it. The cat creature was still to be reckoned with.

Almost at the boy's feet the lake water lapped at the shore. The trail around the lake had dried since he had traveled it a few hours before. Nearing his own camp, Kepa saw his little dog standing worriedly by the sheep he had been told to watch. When the dog saw his master leave the trail for the grass beside the tent and the campfire, he ran to him, jumped up on him, licking the boy's face and hands, saying that he had been faithful to his responsibility—the sheep—but his heart had been with his master. "Tonight we keep double watch, but at tomorrow's dawn we leave this place," Kepa told Keeper, lighting the camp-fire. If it did not rain he would keep it burning through the night. He thought that the wild animal might not come near a campfire, but if it did he could see him better by its light.

20 KEEPER, ALBERTO, AND KEPA sat around the evening campfire. Carlos had sent a piece of venison, a welcome change from sausage and bacon, and the boy had cooked it. They were talking about what had happened since Alberto had come by with the twins. Carlos had been fine when the camp tender had stayed with him last night, but Juan was having trouble. The forest fire on his side of the mountain was spreading and getting too near his band for safety. He had decided to herd his sheep to the rolling hill country, bypassing the area where the fire was raging and making a short cut to where the buyers would be when the herders brought in the lambs to be sold.

"I expected you to be where I left you," Alberto told Kepa, "and not here, two days' distance away. Why did you leave so unexpectedly? There was grass there for four or five days more. What made you decide to go?" Kepa had been hoping for the question and anxious to tell why he had left the meadow.

He told about the animal that had killed the doe, how it looked, how far it could leap, and its way of attack. "Boy!" Alberto said, "You were playing hide-and-seek with a mountain lion, a dangerous animal. It can leap easily twenty feet and kills its prey by jumping on its back and breaking its neck. What happened?" Kepa told how he had tracked the cat and how in turn it had stalked him. The camp tender laughed. "It would not have attacked you unless it was cornered. It was only curious about you, but it would maul your dog and kill your mule first chance it got."

Kepa told next about the storm and the tree's being struck by lightning. "I decided to get out of there." The boy paused, laughing, then continued. "The next morning when the sun was bright and warm and everything was peaceful, I tried to talk myself out of going. Keeper and I were tired. We'd had two nights with scarcely an hour of sleep. Patto-Kak was tired, too, from his night of freedom. I counted all the reasons I should stay. The salt you left had been soaked by the rain, but it was getting dry, and the sheep were eating it. I thought, too, that probably the mountain lion had enough to eat for the next few days. All those reasons to stay but I couldn't find a single reason to go." The boy stopped talking.

"Then why did you go?" the camp tender asked curiously.

"I don't know. Something made me. I got those sheep out of there an hour after dawn."

There was no more talk for awhile. Kepa gave Keeper the venison bone to gnaw. Alberto said, "Funny thing—your going. You know what happened, probably the night of the day you left? A fire started on the opposite side of the lake. Couldn't go across the lake, but the wind must have swept a blaze or two around the lake. Your end of the campsite was burned some-what, but the opposite side was burned bare when I rode through a couple of days ago."

"If I had stayed, what would have happened to the sheep?" Kepa asked in a shaken voice.

"Your guess is as good as mine," Alberto answered, "but I doubt you could have saved them." Then he added, "When one has herded sheep as long as I have, he tends to believe in luck, destiny, or whatever you want to call it. Funny thing your going." Again there was silence.

"Did you have much trouble getting here?" the man asked, probably to change the subject. Kepa laughed. "Did I have trouble getting here? I'll say I did, and I have two sheep tails to prove it." The boy got up to put a new log on the campfire. Campfires, other than for cooking, were luxuries, but so was company. The fire blazed and crackled cheerfully, inviting talk.

"The first noon we stopped in a perfect place," he said. "An aspen grove, grass, wild flowers, a mountain stream, and over-head a roof of dancing aspen leaves, but I wanted to get farther away from the mountain lion, so I pushed on. Just before sunset when we were ready to stop again, we came upon a landslide. A whole piece of a mountain had slid down into the trail. To take that many sheep across it might jar another hunk of moun-tain loose, so I herded them around it." Kepa laughed, remem-bering the experience. "Well, I did it, but it took me half the night almost."

"What happened the second day?" Alberto wanted to know.

Kepa went to put the mule's stake in a new place. When he came back, he said, "Buy me a new tether and put it in the book. That one's too short and frayed to mend." Then he con-tinued, "What happened the second day was worse. It was noon, a warm, sunny day, not a cloud in the sky. Suddenly with no warning at all, hailstones as big as my fist started to hit us from every direction. The sheep went into their circle dance, and before the hail stopped and we could get them separated, one lamb was smothered and one trampled. Keeper and I ate mutton."

"That's herding," the camp tender said. "There's always too much weather. If there isn't too much rain, there's too much drought."

Kepa asked, smiling, "Want to come with me to tell the sheep to sleep well?"

134

"No, they can do without my good-night kiss," Alberto said. "I'm turning in."

Before leaving the next morning the man gave the boy directions for getting down the mountain to where the road met the trail, which was where the buyers would be with their mule-drawn freight wagons to haul the lambs to market. "You have two weeks. Should be easy. There are three good campsites with forage and water along the way. The last one's the prettiest aspen grove you ever saw. Has its own waterfall. The aspen grove and the other sites are on ridges, but one is in a valley. As a general rule you would camp about the same length of time in the three places, but this year is an unusually rainy one, so better plan for longer stays on the ridges."

The pack mules were skittish. They had carried no loads for almost a week and now refused their packsaddles. "Get along there," the camp tender shouted, pulling their saddles tighter and whacking them into their places in the string. At last they were ready to go. The man mounted his horse and sat, looking down at the boy. "I'll probably go with you the last day," he said. "I'll come the night before with your new clothes, the dictionary, and a new lead for Patto-Kak. If you don't mind, think I'll bring along a shears and do a little barber work on your hair. Be nice to see your face again." Alberto started his pack string along the trail, then stopped his horse to call over his shoulder, "Chris said to tell you she'll be seeing you."

Kepa walked swiftly toward the camp tender. "María Cristina? Will she be at the fork where the buyers will be?"

"Sure thing. Chris, her mother, the twins, Pedro—the whole family are coming. My wife too. We leave the babies in Boise, but for the rest of us it will be a family camping party combined with work."

"Oh," Kepa said. "Well, be sure you don't forget to bring the shears."

21 THE LAMBS WERE FAT; even the old ewes looked good. Filled with a sense of well being, Kepa looked around his mountain world. He must be a mountain person, he thought, because he loved the crags and the peaks, the canyons and the valleys, the thick fringe of the forest and the glacial world above the timberline. Yet, thinking back, he decided that he might have loved the desert too, if he had not felt so new and strange and lonely. Its vast, empty, barren space had been so foreign to the people-filled world of his Basque homeland. When he went through it again this winter maybe it, too, would have its own beauty. The boy stretched lazily in the warm sunshine, giving a glance at his sheep and a pat to his dog.

Nearly every day now there was a brief rain, enough to freshen the world and upset the sheep. When the sun came out again, they placidly went about their business of eating and resting and eating. As for himself, he liked the rain as well as the sunshine.

The boy examined his notched stick. Tonight he would put the sixth notch in it. Almost a week, he thought, since Alberto had been with him, and now only a week more to go. Tomorrow would be time to move on and if all went well, tomorrow night they would be camping in the valley. Perhaps he would stay there three days and then go up to the next ridge. Finally, at the sixth notch on the second stick Alberto would come with the new clothes, and Kepa, his dog, his mule, and the sheep would go winding down the mountain. The fat young lambs and the fat, old ewes would be sold to the buyers and hauled in the wagons to the railroad. He would see his godfather and Juan and Carlos—all of them. And Cristina.

Kepa looked at his collection of carved figures. The mountain goat and the racoon were right. He was pleased with them. Then he looked at the unfinished mountain lion; the head, the forefeet, the lean, long body, looked like the animal he had seen, but not the hindquarters. He could not carve them because he had not seen them. "I think I'll let this one stay unfinished," he told Keeper. The dog opened an eye questioningly, but knowing that his master was only talking and not giving a command, went back to sleep again.

Each morning a stag had made a brief stop to look over his domain and decide if this was the day he should go forth to conquer it. Kepa had tried carving its image, but he did not like what he had done. He had not been able to catch the animal's strength and pride. How could one catch an inner spirit and make it live in a piece of wood, he wondered. Yet he must do it because pride and strength were as much a part of the stag he saw as was the flesh and bone of the magnificent animal.

The daily rain began and the sheep scattered. "The rain will stop as soon as we get the silly beasts rounded up," he told Keeper. But the rain did not stop; it came down in a slow and steady drizzle all afternoon and evening and night.

The next morning the rain was still dripping from a leaden sky. There was neither wind nor thunder nor lightning and no sign of sun, just the steady drip of rain and rain and rain.

Another day would overgraze the ridge where he was camping. He would go on. The boy decided not to waste time trying to build a campfire. He and Keeper would eat cold food again this morning.

The sheep disliked rain. When it rained they neither wanted to browse nor to be herded. Their respect for and probably fear of the dog was the only reason that they moved at all. Once on the way, again and again they stampeded, trying to go back to the place they remembered as safe. The trail was cloud-filled, misting the sheep and the trees into unreal, gray ghost figures. Patto-Kak was unruly, continually jerking his lead rope and trying to rid himself of packsaddle and load.

At noon the sun shone through the clouds, but the trees and the plants and the grass remained dripping and water-soaked. Even the air was heavy with moisture, and the sheep rested fitfully. Kepa decided on another cold lunch. "This evening, rain or shine," he promised Keeper, "we will have hot food. We will be forced to make a fire and cook. All the food that is left is raw."

Rain began again and the sheep started scattering uphill, as usual. "That is the wrong way," Kepa yelled at them furiously. "You stupid beasts, can't you understand that we are trying to go downhill into the valley?" If the stupid beasts understood, they paid no attention to their herder's shouting, heeding only the nips of the little dog.

Shortly after sunset they were where Kepa planned they would be—in the valley. It was not a wide one and its hillsides were rather steep, but there was grass and a shallow stream, bordered with willow and cottonwood trees. It would be adequate for three, perhaps four days' grazing.

Kepa made the seventh notch in his stick and discarded it. Tomorrow he would get a new stick, and by its seventh notch he would be where the lambs were to be sold.

The rain stopped, but the sky remained cloudy. Still, there

138

would be perhaps an hour of daylight left, enough for Kepa to unload, hobble the mule, put up the tent, and chop dry wood for the evening fire. He could cook, if need be, by lantern light. "I should cook enough for tomorrow," he told Patto-Kak, and at the mule's indignant squealing at being hobbled, he said, "I'm sorry, but if it rains tonight, I must stand guard. I cannot take the time to move your stake from place to place."

Before the meal was cooked, it was raining again. The wood was dry but the fire smoked and sputtered, and the boy had a hard time trying to keep the flame alive. He and his dog ate by lantern light. Then they walked among the sheep. They were restless tonight. Keeper also was restless, bounding away at every imagined disturbance. Along with the patter of rain on the tent, the bushes, and the trees, Kepa could hear the clink and the soft thump of the hobbles and his mule's feet on the wet grass as he hobbled back and forth, back and forth, through the grass and the night.

By dawn, there still was no sun in the cloud-heavy sky. The restlessness of the dog, the mule, and the sheep had communicated an unease to the shepherd. The rain still fell, not in the fury of a storm but in a steady, slow, incessant drip, as if it never would stop. The entire valley became cloud-filled, and even the sloping hills did not exit. "We're getting out of here now," Kepa said loudly, more to reassure himself than to inform the sheep.

Packing took longer than he had anticipated. Everything was waterlogged, heavy, and difficult to handle. His bedroll was soggy, his canvas tent stiff and as hard as a board, making it almost impossible to take down and roll into a small, tight bundle. Patto-Kak bucked off his packsaddle, a feat he had been trying to accomplish for four months. The sheep stampeded.

It was midmorning before they were actually on the move across the valley. As they started, the sun broke through the clouds making a rainbow arch above the moving band. Almost immediately the clouds hid the sun again. The rainbow faded and the gray day folded itself around them.

Far up the valley, the dull sky became filled with a yellow-green gigantic cloud hanging over it. The sheep began running up the embankment. The mule jerked his rope with such un-expected force that Kepa let it slip from his hand. Keeper began to bark furiously, nipping the legs of the sheep that always trailed at the end of the band. The rest of the band were stream-ing uphill and some had reached the top. Lightning tore the sky into ribbons as clap after clap of thunder hit the distant moun-tain peaks and rebounded in echos. Then came a roar louder and more prolonged than thunder as the yellow-green cloud burst from its own weight and a wall of water over six feet high came flooding the stream and the entire valley floor.

Kepa had never seen or heard of a wall of water rushing in fury and violence into a narrow little valley, but he lost no time in looking or wondering. Instinctively he looked at his sheep and the ones almost over the ridge and the ones trailing at the edge of the water. Keeper was running at their heels nipping them frantically, urging them up the embankment. As Kepa looked, the wall of water broke, churning and crested with yellow foam, gaining in force and volume.

The boy had time for one thing only, to save Keeper. Drop-ping his staff, he grabbed his dog, throwing him across his shoulders as the old shepherd had done with the lambs he carried on the mountaintop of the Pyrenees. The dog did not struggle but lay quietly. He helps me even in this, Kepa thought, as he ran from the water that pulled against his feet and slapped against his body, threatening to pull him into its wild flooding.

Gaining the ridge at last, he put the dog on the ground. The small, plucky animal ran after the sheep, nipping them to the safety of the ridge and its high, peaceful meadow, as if being carried from the water's peril was his master's work, while his work was to safeguard the sheep.

Kepa looked down at the flooded valley, now a wide river, carrying along in its raging flood uprooted pine and cotton-wood trees and huge boulders that turned and bobbed and swirled in the powerful current. There was no sign of the sheep that had trailed the band.

As he looked down at the raging waters of the flood, the boy thought of the tagalongs, as he called them. There were six, and since his first day of herding they had been a worry and an irritation. They were always trailing. Even if accidentally they were pushed in the middle of the band, they got back to their places at the end as soon as possible. Because they had been such nuisances, always lagging or straying or taking their time when he wanted them to hurry, he had known them very well as individual animals, not as just a part of the band. Now that they were gone, he would miss them.

Kepa looked at the sheep that were walking reluctantly in the rain. There were still almost twenty-five hundred of them he thought, trying to comfort himself for the loss of the six tag-alongs. The last two weeks had been difficult on the dispositions but not on the weight of the sheep. "You are in good condi-tion," he told them, "you fat, woolly, stupid, mud-colored, stubborn creatures."

Then he remembered his mule. Where was Patto-Kak? Had he been dashed to pieces by the boulders and uprooted trees being swept down the flooded valley? Kepa felt sick. "He was my friend," he kept saying over and over. "He was my friend. We liked each other." The boy looked down at the raging river. There could be no way to save his mule even if he could see him in the debris-filled water. He stooped to pick up his shepherd's crook, then remembered that he had dropped it when he rescued Keeper.

Blindly the young herder went on. He must follow his flock. No matter what happened, the sheep must come first. As he walked through the wet grass of the meadow in the beating rain, his thoughts were of home in the Spanish Basque land. He remembered the day the old shepherd had given him his *makela,* the shepherd's staff.

He had not been surprised. He knew the Old One had been making it for him. When Kepa, three years before, had first herded his sheep in the high summer pasture, he had helped the shepherd select the tree that he would use to make the *makela.* They had hunted a long time before they found it. It had to be a special kind of tree and a perfect specimen of its kind. At last they had found such a tree. It had not more than a year's growth, was slender-trunked and straight, supple, and strong.

The boy had watched the shepherd notch its bark with line cuts, making a kind of design that would designate it as Kepa's staff for the years of his life to come. When the bark had been cut to the Old One's liking, Kepa had helped him wrap the trunk with strips of strong cloth so that the tree's running sap would fill the incisions in the bark and in time harden and make a permanent design.

Last autumn, after Kepa had taken his flock from the mountain pasture down to the valley *caserío* for winter, the old shepherd had felled the tree, now in its fourth year of growth, still slender and straight. He had soaked it in a solution of tree ashes and water to darken it. Then he heated it in the little stove where he baked his bread to harden it until it was strong as steel. At last, he had tested the new *makela,* and it had passed the test. He was satisfied. It had taken four years to fashion, but the staff would last a lifetime and longer.

Kepa remembered the day the old shepherd had given him the staff, before he had left his father's house to go to the new world of Idaho, America. He remembered also the last time he had seen the beloved Old One.

At the last turn in the trail he had seen the old man standing under an oak tree, waiting for him to pass by. Seeing him standing there, Kepa suddenly knew that here was another dear companion who was too old, too tired to walk the trail to the village and back again to his mountaintop. The old shepherd raised his staff. Kepa raised his. It was their greeting and their farewell. "Go on. Go on," Kepa commanded his feet. "Do not stop. Do not make it more difficult for him. Make your farewell quickly and completely. Do not look back." Instead, the boy looked at his staff. It was his strength and his shield. He would keep it always.

Now it was gone!

At last the rain stopped and the sun shone brightly as if ashamed of the havoc the storm had wrought. The sheep were quietly browsing, having forgotten their panic of an hour ago. Then Kepa saw Patto-Kak at the far side of the meadow, as jaunty as ever. The boy sat down on the soppy ground and looked at his mule and his sheep. Keeper came back to lick his master's face, trying to tell him that danger was now behind them. "You and Patto-Kak are safe," Kepa told him. "And when I go back to Spain maybe the old shepherd will make me another *makela.*"

**22** KEPA HERDED THE BAND OF SHEEP down the wooded slope toward the place where the road met the trail and the buyers would look over the lambs. The late summer day was a perfect one, still and bright and warm, but with an under-lay of autumn coolness in the air. August with its rain and thunderstorms, its forest fires, cloudbursts, and flood, was in its last week. The rainy season lay behind the young herder like a tree-blazed trail. Each blaze, as each happening, had been a small but sharp-edged cut that healed slowly and left a lasting scar, each scar a blaze, each blaze a marker showing the way he had traveled and probably would travel again.

As today was, so had been the week just passed, each day sun-drenched and golden. The wild flowers, in sudden frenzy that winter was on its way, burst into fuller bloom, trying to prolong their loveliness. Each sunrise the birds flitting about in the tree-tops rivaled their neighbor birds in song and joined them in reverent evensong at twilight.

The summer rainy season was all but ended, and the daily showers lessened in quantity, intensity, and length. Each night came earlier, stayed later, wrapping the land in a velvet cape studded with a million stars.

144

Alberto had come much sooner than Kepa had expected. He explained that Juan's mule had a badly cut leg and he was tak-ing him another mule. He could stay with Kepa only long enough for the promised haircut and to share the noonday meal. "Will you take Juan's mule back to the ranch?" Kepa asked.

Alberto shrugged. "Depends on how deep the cut is."

"How did it happen?" Again the man shrugged. "Who knows? About this time of year, Juan gets homesick. Anything can happen."

Realizing that he had been asking questions only to put off telling about his own loss, Kepa suddenly told the story of the drowned tailers. This time he felt neither shame nor embarrass-ment at the loss of his employer's sheep. It was neither careless-ness nor bad judgment on his part. There was no way, he thought, that the loss could have been avoided. Evidently, Alberto was of the same opinion. He said, "That's part of sheep business—losses. Sheep, dog, mules, even the herders themselves can be wiped out at a turn of the wind or the weather."

Kepa nodded. "Wind and weather," he said musingly. "I suppose unusually rainy seasons as this one has been are the worst."

"No," Alberto answered, "the worst year for a herder to en-dure is the unusually dry year. It's a terrible thing to have to walk with your band day after day watching them slowly die from thirst and hunger. It's a terrible thing to know that you have left the trail behind marked with the bleached bones of sheep that were under your care." Alberto finished drinking his coffee. "Well," he said, "you have three days to get there. Better move them tomorrow and then make a two-night camp at the aspen grove with the waterfall." The man got his horse and stood looking at the resting sheep. He said, "Good work, boy. I'm proud of you. The best-conditioned band I've seen in many a moon. Twenty-five hundred sheep."

"Not quite. I've lost almost a dozen," Kepa said.

"How old are you?" the man asked suddenly.

"Sixteen, I'll be seventeen just before Christmas. In case you think I'm not very old, remember I'm a stubborn Basque," Kepa answered. "We are all stubborn Basque or we wouldn't be here." The camp tender laughed, riding away, leading a reluctant mule behind him.

That had been three days ago. Patto-Kak was grazing, the sheep were bedded for the night. Kepa and his dog walked to a lookout point where he could see the camp at the place where the road met the trail. The camp far below them at the foot of the mountain looked unreal and toylike. There were four tents. One of them, Kepa thought, was Rosa's cook tent. It had been pitched before the cook fire and had a row of Dutch ovens before the open flap. There were a dozen or more pole corrals with chutes connecting some of them. They would be for the sheep, he knew, because already there were ewes in one of them and lamb in another. At one end were two other corrals. In one of them there were five saddle horses. Cristina had been right when she said they had good horses at the ranch. These were beautiful. Kepa, squatting on the ground, looked down at them and lambs in another. At one end were two other corrals. his godfather and the two fat pinto ponies, which were the twins' mounts. The boy looked around the encampment, wondering who would ride the fifth horse. Someday, maybe, he thought wistfully, he would own a horse, "to match the gold watch I'll buy." He laughed at the wild thought of such an extravagant dream.

Suddenly he saw the twins. Carlos has come then, he thought, and it is his band I saw in the two corrals. The boy crawled to the edge of the lookout point, hanging over the edge, trying to see if Carlos' lambs were fatter than his own. He could not be certain.

146

A car came down the road and stopped by the tents. It was his godfather's car, the one he had ridden in from Boise to the ranch. Cristina's mother and Rosa got out. "The mother can drive a car?" the boy said aloud in wonder. "She drives a car alone on the road?" It was difficult to believe.

Cristina came out of her tent to greet her mother and Rosa. Godfather Pedro came from another tent, and the twins came running from the corral to the automobile. Instantly Kepa turned away. They were such a happy family, he felt he had no place with them. He did not belong. "I am stupid," he scolded. "Godfather is First Neighbor's son and I am his namesake, also." But even though he reasoned thusly, he did not go back to the lookout point.

Far on a trail below the mountain he saw another band slowly moving toward the little circle of corrals and tents. This band would be Juan's, he thought, noting that there were two men walking with the sheep and leading a horse and two mules, and one of the mules he could see was lame.

Because they were hungry, the boy and the dog enjoyed the evening meal. Kepa lighted the lantern and unwrapped the dictionary the camp tender had brought him. For a long time he turned the pages, studying the words. At last he looked up, satisfied. He had learned the words and he was going to make himself say them. Now he practiced saying them aloud, "Good morning. Happiness I have to see you."

Kepa and Keeper and Patto-Kak and the sheep wakened at the first hint of morning sunrise in the sky. Last night there had been the first breath of autumn, turning every leaf and plant to crimson and gold. In the bright morning sunlight the leaves and blades of grass sparkled with new frost as if they had been sprinkled with stardust.

In an hour Kepa's band was moving down the mountain. The pack mule, wearing his load like an emperor's cloak, led the sheep as he had been doing since the day of the flood. Almost twenty-five hundred sheep followed him docilely down the trail. Patto-Kak led them; Keeper nipped them; and Kepa, proudly wearing his new American-made clothes, walked behind them, watching over them.

**23** THREE HECTIC DAYS WENT BY. They reminded Kepa of the shearing season during his first days at the ranch when out of confusion, noise, dust, smells, sweat, and work came order and efficiency.

Carlos' lambs and some of the older ewes of his band were weighed, sorted, sold, and freighted by mule-drawn wagons to the nearest railroad station. This done, Carlos took his band, now about a third of its original size, back into the mountains where they would stay until the first golden weeks of October to begin their trek across the desert to the home ranch for lambing.

Juan had been the second one in, so he was the second one for the buyers to make their bids for buying his lambs. The only rule that held for the herders was an unwritten one. The herder who was first on the trail had his choice of trails, of rangelands and water. The first at headquarters for lambing was first to use the sheds. In everything the first one was first. The rule was never disputed.

The condition of one band of sheep was never compared with the condition of another herder's band, that is, not officially, not by the Boss, but every herder knew. Kepa, though a beginner, knew by the end of the first day which herder had the fattest lambs. He was very quiet about it, but also very pleased. He thought of the old shepherd at home in the Pyrenees and wished he could tell the Old One about the boy he had trained and given the shepherd's staff. He wished he could tell Tío Marco that his band had kept to the standard he had set for them.

Lamb-selling time is work time, not a holiday, but when as many as two Basque get together there is merrymaking and an exchange of letters and gossip. So it was now. There were letters from family and friends for all three of the herders. Kepa's was from his father. His news was sad. The old shepherd and Tinka, he had written, had both gone the trail of no returning. Both on the same night, both at the *caserío*. Carmen, father said, had gone up to the mountaintop to bring the Old One down for her wedding. He had come gladly, but he never went back to his mountain world again. At the end of father's letter, Little Mother had written her words of comfort. "Do not grieve for them, dear son. They were old and they were tired and where-ever they are, they are together, Tinka guarding the Old One from danger and the Old One protecting Tinka from harm." Kepa put the letter back in its envelope. He remembered his last talk when the old man had told him, "I know you will come back to the land of the Basque sometime, some year, but I will not be here to greet you. I am too old. I, too, face a new trail that soon will coax my feet to walk it." His father had been right, Kepa thought, when he said that home, when you return, is not the same as when you left it.

The boy remembered the last time he and Tinka had gone to the pasture to fork bundles of dry grass for the cow and the donkey. That had been his last time to feed them, these animal friends who had been a part of his life for as long as he could remember. That had been his hour to say good-bye to the things of his boyhood, the encircling trees, the wooded hills, the rugged peaks that belonged to him and he to them. Kepa, who had been thinking of the Old One just the day before, had a moment of comfort. Perhaps the old shepherd had known what the boy wanted him to know. As for Tinka, in a way Tinka would always be with him in his love for Keeper.

At last the buyers looked at Kepa's band. They bought all of the fat, old ewes and three fourths of the fat, young lambs. They would have bought all the lambs, but Godfather Pedro always kept some of the best to breed for next year's lamb crop.

At tomorrow's dawn Kepa planned to take his now much smaller band back over the trail they had come down three days ago.

Godfather's family, Alberto and his wife, Rosa, and Kepa were sitting around the campfire. Kepa had not had an opportunity to say, "Good morning. Happiness I have to see you," in English to Cristina. He had not seen her alone to talk to, and saying it before an audience took more bravery than he possessed. They had been singing Diego's songs, the older people as well as the younger ones. The scene reminded Kepa of winter nights at home with his and First Neighbor's family.

At the end of one of the songs, Godfather Pedro said, "Chris tells me that our herder Kepa worries because he cannot turn in the six tails from the sheep that drowned in the flood." There was silence. Everyone waited for Pedro to continue. Kepa felt uneasy. He had not told Cristina that he was worried about the missing tails. What is she up to? he wondered. After a proper time of silence, Pedro said, "Chris tells me that if she has her parents' permission to take the horses and ride with young Kepa, she thinks she knows where to look for the sheep to get their tails."

It sounds like a family conference at the *caserío;* Godfather is teasing, Kepa thought. This isn't the way people act in

America. Cristina's little mother will not permit it. Young ladies do not ride alone with young men.

The camp tender said, "I certainly need those sheep tails for tally."

Rosa spoke as if she were speaking to herself, "I could give them a picnic lunch and not have to pack all that food back to the ranch."

It was the twins' turn to speak. "We haven't anything special to do tomorrow. We could go with them."

The last suggestion seemed to be the winning one. María Cristina's mother laughed, a low tinkle of amusement. "I'm certain the poor sheep will be somewhere, waiting to give up their tails." She smiled at Cristina. How much they look alike, Kepa thought. Almost as much as the twins look like each other. The mother continued, "How sad for Kepa to be so worried, how thoughtful of our three children to try to help him." Now it was Cristina's turn to smile at her mother. Everyone waited.

"Yes? Little Mother?" Pedro prodded gently.

"*Como no*," the little mother answered gaily. "Since her brothers are so willing to go with them, María Cristina may help our Kepa hunt sheep's tails."

"Thank you, Mother," Cristina said dutifully.

Pedro had a word for Kepa. "Chris is the best sheepman in the family," he boasted, "but sometimes she lets her imagination run away with what she knows is fact. Don't plan, my son, on finding either the sheep or their tails."

Kepa could feel his blood burning his neck and his face. He knew as well as Pedro that they could not find the sheep. Besides, he had not told Cristina that he wanted their tails. He had not talked with her, not even to say the English sentences he had learned. But what could he say? Nothing! One did not contradict a lady, even a young one.

Cristina's mother said softly, "Walk with me, Kepa." When

she saw the boy draw back in shyness, she said, "There has been so much talk today. I need the stillness of the stars." She took his arm lightly and they walked into the starlit night.

Rosa also spoke softly. "But Chris, such a poor excuse to take the boy horseback riding. I know why you did it."

Chris's eyes filled with tears. "He never gets to do anything like other boys his age, just work and walk. We ride, but he walks." Rosa answered reasonably, "He's a Basque. Basque do not mind walking. Your father walked for many years to give you your chance to ride."

"Yes," Chris said, "My father walked and my mother cried as I am crying." She went into her tent.

**24** "DO YOU RIDE WESTERN OR SPANISH SADDLE?" Chris asked Kepa at the corral where she and her brothers had been waiting for him.

"This is your horse," one twin said, and the other one added, "Chris chose this one from all the others." The horse they were talking about was the extra one Kepa had watched from his lookout point on the trail. "Chris brought him on lead all the way from Boise. Dad rode with her but she led your horse," the twins reported.

"Spanish," Kepa answered Chris's question and then asked, "How did you know about my sheep being swept away in the flood?"

"She has spies, all over the mountains," the twins told him.

Chris laughed, flicking her quirt at her brothers. "Did you get our lunch?" she asked them.

"Yes, the saddlebags are full."

"Enough for an army."

As usual, one twin spoke first, and the other one added whatever was needed. The twins and Cristina like each other; they are friends, Kepa thought, looking at the girl and her younger brothers. Like Paco and Manuel were with me.

154

Godfather and his wife and Alberto and Rosa came to the corral to speed the riders on their way. "Keeper is with my sheep," Kepa said worriedly, "I've never left him for a whole day before."

"He would be worried if he did not stay with the sheep," Pedro said, and Alberto added, "The rest will be good for him."

There was another worry in Kepa's mind. "Godfather, in case we need one, who is the shepherd of this flock?"

"You are," Pedro spoke unhesitatingly, pleased that the boy felt a responsibility for the others.

"Do you hear that?" Kepa asked the twins.

"Yes, we hear it."

At first Kepa felt shy. This was the first time he had been only with young people. In the Basque country there were many merrymaking occasions, but along with the young people were older cousins and aunts and uncles as well as parents.

Chris, sensing his shyness, had a remedy for it. "For most of the day we will be on the trail you came down, so you can show it to us." She did not mention that she as well as the twins knew the trail also, and at a look from their sister the twins had nothing to say. Kepa in his eagerness to show them where he had camped and what he had seen forgot his shyness and his responsibility for their safety and became their good companion.

When the trail was narrow and steep, Chris rode first in line, followed single file by her brothers and Kepa, but many places were wide enough for two horses to walk abreast. Then Chris dropped behind to ride with Kepa. "I saw this horse from my lookout point above your camp," he confided, "but I didn't know I'd be the one to ride it." Chris did not answer. She had known he would be the one who would ride the horse, but she had not known how she would manage it until Alberto had told her about the lost sheep.

At noon, they reached an aspen grove where last night's frost had turned each dancing aspen leaf to gold. The blueberry bushes were heavy with fruit. The piñon trees were dropping their cones of sweet piñon nuts, and the squirrels were scampering about gathering and storing their winter's supply. There was the special early autumn smell that comes to the high places at summer's end, and the air was filled with the scent of resin that came from the bruised pine needles in the trail that the horses' hooves had trod upon.

"I know this place," Kepa exclaimed, "I night-camped here the night after the flood."

"Let's rest here. We're hungry," the twins said, reining in their horses.

"No, let's go on a bit. I know where my cook fire was. Right in back of it was a waterfall."

Around a slight curve in the trail they came upon the remembered campsite, the bough bed, the flat stones of the cook fire, and the place where the sheep had bedded down. Today the camp was occupied. There was a tiny fire between the two flat stones and a coffee pot on one of them. Busily grazing nearby was a gray-colored burro. Chris and Kepa spoke at the same time. "Hans," Chris called. "The prospector," Kepa said in surprised delight.

Although Chris and Kepa were the first to speak, the twins, sliding from their horses, were the first to reach the dust-colored old man sitting at one side of the fire. The old man hugged the two young boys, but his first words were for Kepa. "I've been waiting for you to come, lad, four days. I brought you the sheep tails and your herder's staff. It also was carried downstream, but as you see, it is not broken."

Kepa felt tears sting his eyes. He had not expected to see his shepherd's crook again. "You got them for me? You've been waiting all these days for me to come? My *makela* is safe?" The boy knew he was babbling but it was such a surprise. He had thought he would never see his staff again.

The old man spoke to Chris, "Ah, lass, that you should cross my trail today."

"Hans," Chris spoke softly. "Dear Hans, you know I am always glad to see you."

The twins brought the saddlebags and Chris fixed the lunch Rosa had packed for them. As they ate they asked the old pros-pector questions. "I saw the flood from high up on the mountain, but I could not get across the water-filled valley to help you, so," he said simply, "I did the next best thing. Waited a day for the flood to spend itself, then went downstream until I found what was left of the sheep. Found the crook, I did, lodged in a cedar as if someone put it there for safekeeping."

The twins were big-eyed with wonder. "How did you get the sheep? Did you swim in after them?" they wanted to know.

"Waded through the mud," Hans explained. "Water from a flash flood like that drains off quickly. Their bodies were wedged between uprooted trees and boulders. Took a might of prying and digging."

"Dear Hans," Chris said again, smiling at the old man.

Kepa remembered the carved box and what Tío had said about it. He looked at Chris curiously and wondered if she really did look like the picture of the young girl Hans had kept for so many years. Chris, sensing his look, said, "You wonder why Hans and I know each other? I've known Hans since I was a very little girl. We've always been friends."

"Her dad grub-outfits me every year, but Chris and her mother give me the little extras that I like," the prospector ex-plained. "Chris and the twins always seem to know where I'm going to be. Bring me things wherever I am."

The twins had been quiet long enough. Now they felt they had to speak. "Hans gave Chris her dog."

"The one that's Keeper's mother."

"That's right," the little gnomelike man said cheerfully. "Told her I couldn't feed it properly. Wanted it to have the home it deserved." Kepa looked quickly at Chris. The young girl was smiling, but her eyes held the secret of sadness.

Talk turned to other things. The twins told about their time with Carlos. Kepa decided he liked the twins. They were good workers and were fun to have around. As for Chris, she had his sister Carmen's efficiency and María's gentleness and something else also. Something that probably America had given her. The boy was quiet, trying to find the word to describe the "something else." Finally he found the perfect word—companionship. "You are a good companion," he told her. "A good companion."

Hans agreed. "For the long trail she can lead or follow or walk beside, whichever is needed."

"Time to pack," Chris told the twins.

The old man went to his pack for some of the small sacks, which Chris filled with the food that was left. The twins helped Kepa bank the fire with damp earth so there would be no spark for the wind to spread. Hans handed Kepa the sheep tails and the crook, which Chris took and looked at in silence. Then handing them to Kepa, she spoke to Hans, "I had not expected to meet you here. I had not expected to find anything left of the sheep. It's . . . it's important, as if it was meant to be."

"I was waiting for the lad to come, not you. First time I've ever known you to come to watch the lambs being freighted away," Hans told her. "Many things are meant to be, lassie, if we could read the signs."

The twins were examining the shepherd's crook. "A regular *makela,* from the Basque country."

"How did you get it?"

"Tell us about it."

"Another time," Kepa told them. He did not want anyone

to know how grateful he was to have the Old One's gift back again. If I could read the signs, he thought, maybe I'm meant to be a herder of sheep.

"Now," Hans said, cackling with laughter, "I've a present for you, a memory to take away with you. A memory," he told them seriously, "is the only thing you can't spend or lose or have stolen. This memory is for you to keep."

Nearby the water of the little creek tumbled down over the rocks to its bed a hundred feet below, making a light waterfall of white-crested lace. Placing his forefinger against his lips in a gesture for silence, the old man led them climbing down the rocky ledge beside the waterfall. When they had reached the creek bed below, he again motioned for silence and led them through an opening beside the fall into a huge cavelike room, its high, rounded walls moss-covered and its opening a curtain spray of gauze.

As their eyes became accustomed to the darkness of the cave, they saw that the pool, a stone's throw from the twinkling water of the fall, was crystal clear. Speckled silver trout leaped high into the air and dived back into the pool's transparent depth, making an arch of iridescent color. The gentle roar of the falling water reverberating against the rock wall of the cave had a hollow, unreal sound that was felt rather than heard.

The twins moved closer to Chris and she put her arm protectingly about their shoulders. Kepa felt her movement rather than saw it and he stepped back instinctively, not wanting to intrude into the family circle. At once, Chris put her free hand in his, reminding him of a little girl asking protection of some older, trusted person.

Hans made another motion for silence although none of them had breathed a sound. They waited a long time. It seemed to Kepa a precious time of his being a member of First Neighbor's family.

There was a crashing sound and a thrashing about in the

bushes and trees at the far side of the pool. Lumbering awk-wardly through the underbrush came a big brown bear nosing her cub before her into the icy water. Kepa caught his breath. The curtain of falling water misted the figures, softening without blurring them.

The mother bear stood upright and with the speed of light-ning she snatched a leaping trout in her great cumbersome paw. The young cub, watching his mother, also stood upright, snatched at a diving trout, missed it, then sat down in the swirl-ing water with a look of bewildered outrage. Looking as if she wanted to console her cub for his loss of the fish, the huge bear mother broke branches from the trees beside the pool and be-gan juggling them for his amusement. Tired of juggling, she tossed the branches into the pool and both bears watched them bob and swirl. Finally the mother caught them again and, as if saying she was tired of childish play, threw them on the rocky ledge and nosed her young cub out of the pool and into the underbrush.

The play had taken perhaps ten minutes, but when Hans led them out of the cave to climb the rock ledge to the aspen grove above, Kepa felt he had been a lifetime away from the reality of his world.

"Did you see the love that mother showed for her cub?" Chris asked breathlessly.

"Could the bear have harmed us, cornered as we were in the cave?" Kepa asked, mindful that he was shepherd of this small flock.

Old Hans looked at Chris, nodding in agreement, but his answer was for Kepa. "Lad," he said reprovingly, "I tested the wind with my finger first. She could not get our scent."

The twins asked, "How did you know they'd be there? Does she come every day?" They still were seeing the great brown bear, ferocious and feared, amusing her small cub, consoling him for his loss of a fish.

"At this time of year they often come to the pool," Hans said.

Kepa put the sheep tails in one of the saddlebags and the shepherd's crook under his arm. "I'll never be able to thank you properly for all you have done today," he told the prospector. "Or for the memory, dear Hans," Chris added. The twins said nothing, but as they rode down the trail they raised their arms in a gesture of farewell.

The old man watched them go, the twins leading, Chris next, and Kepa last in line. The old prospector stopped the boy as he was about to ride by. "Wait, lad. What I do will take but a minute. You can catch up with them before they come to the turn in the trail. Wondered all these years why I toted that box around with me everywhere I went. Now I think I know." Still talking, the Old One took the carved box from his load, opened it, and spread the contents on the ground beside him— family pictures, passports, legal documents, certificates of award. He put them to one side. "These will start my campfire tomorrow morning," he mumbled. "I'll end my days as I have lived them, a man of mystery, going everywhere, getting nowhere." Two things were left, the picture of a young woman and a small wrapped packet. These he handled tenderly, looking at them for a long time. "The dream I could not make come true and cannot forget." He put the picture and the packet back into the box, closed the lid, and motioned for Kepa to go.

Kepa was confused, bewildered. He did not know what the old man had done, or why he had done it. Yet he had a strange feeling that what he had heard and seen was important to him, Kepa, that it would influence his life in some way.

Again Hans motioned for him to go. Knowing that he was dismissed, the boy spurred his horse to catch up with Chris and her brothers.

Shadows filled the aspen grove, wrapping the golden leaves in the gray light of dusk.

5th Part

# TRAILING OUT

**25** THE TIME HAD COME to leave the wilderness area, to trail out over the rolling hills, through the desert sands back to the home camp for lambing time.

September slipped quietly into October. The ram master had come with the buck herd and the sheep had been bred. The silly lambs that but a few short months ago had played and scampered over the hills now walked the trails as sedate year-lings.

The aspen of the high places and the cottonwood of the val-ley had long been turned to gold, rivaling in their brilliant color the crimson and the russet of the ground oak leaves. As the sheep in the early summer had followed the line of melting snow, so now they preceded the line of new-fallen snow down into the desert rangeland.

The nights were clear and still and cold and the morning nippy, with every plant and shrub, every piñon and cedar crusted with frost, like a heavy sprinkling of broken stars. Mid-day was sunwashed and warm, but darkness came swiftly, bring-ing night's bitter cold. There was no twilight, no lingering of a reluctant sun to bed down in the western sky. There was no brilliant sunrise to herald the dawn of day. There was day and there was night, and the nights were longer than the days.

Trailing out was easier for Kepa than trailing in had been. This time he had been over the trail before. He knew where the creeks and springs and waterholes were, where the willow grew and the grass was thickest. Every night camp brought its memory of the time he had been there before. In the last half year the boy had grown in strength and confidence. This time he knew he could meet the challenges of the trail with courage and judgment. He knew, if need be, he could meet success as well as cope with failure. He was not lonely now. Why should I be? he asked himself. I have my dog and my mule. He loved Keeper with a simple and steadfast devotion, and the dog returned it. Patto-Kak amused and delighted him. Arrogantly the mule led the band, and the fat ewes and the sedate yearlings placidly followed him. The mule was a good leader with a canny way of avoiding rocky precipices and steep embankments. The animal still bucked and kicked and tried to bite his young master when the notion struck him. "But your heart isn't in it," Kepa laughingly told him. "Both of us know you don't mean it."

In early October the band had reached the rolling hills again. This time the hills did not seem to be high, piled on higher hills going upward and seeming never to reach the top. This time the boy knew that at the top of the hills were the forests at the foot of the glacial mountains. He knew that now these lay in back of him. This time he knew that although the desert before him was bleak and barren and empty, it was not eternal. At one end were the mountains and at the other end was the home ranch.

Alberto came on his scheduled trip, leaving supplies and salt and a letter from the twins. Kepa, with an occasional help from Alberto, read it aloud. "This is in English. Basque has too many letters in the words," the twins wrote. "We send you a present so you can know where you are. The months and the days are written in English so you can learn them right. P.S. Chris is making you something for Christmas. The first was not good, so your mother in Spain wrote to her how. Maybe they will get better. P.S.2. We will make you something for Christmas if we can think what." It was signed T. and T.

Kepa opened the gift, which was a calendar the twins had made. There was a pencil tied to it and each numbered blank square was large enough to write in it. Kepa was pleased. Now he would know with certainty where he was as to month and week and day. Not only that, he thought, but now he could plan ahead for where he wanted to be at Christmastime when Cristina would send him what she had made. He asked, "In America, do you exchange gifts at Christmas?" When Alberto nodded, Kepa said, "In Spain it's a church day, but. . . ." He shrugged. "I am in America now." Privately he planned to carve a bear and her cub for María Cristina to keep the memory of the aspen grove and the waterfall. "Do you think the twins would like one of my little carved animals, or the ten rattles from the snake I shot?" he asked anxiously. The camp tender laughed. "Those little bandits will like anything they get."

"Maybe I'll give both the rattles and a carving," the boy decided.

The calendar, Kepa discovered, was much better than a notched stick. According to its markings, the middle of October had arrived. Good. If all went well he could get to the hidden valley by November first and stay there four days before beginning the trek across the windy, barren desert to the ranch.

The boy and his dog walked among the browsing sheep. The band was only half the size it had been before the old ewes and most of the lambs had been sold, but already the sheep had chosen their places in it. There were the bellwethers, the black sheep, the leaders, the middlers, and the tailers, just as there had been in the larger band. "I must take special care of you tailers," he told a fat ewe at the end of the line. As usual, when the boy spoke, Keeper looked up at him and wagged a friendly tail.

The days passed pleasantly enough, but because of the shorter daylight hours, the going was a little slower. Kepa did not know what to do about this. Once he had missed a night camp by almost half a day. Next year, maybe, I will be able to plan better, he thought and upon this thought quickly there came another one. Next year? Would he be here next year or at home in the Pyrenees? He wondered how he would like the Basque country after knowing this wild, fierce land. "I'll love it as I always have," he said aloud and then more softly added, "But I'll miss Idaho, America. I think I'll always miss it." Another thought nagged him, but this one he pushed back. He would not permit it to express itself in words or permit himself to think of it, but he stooped down to give his dog an unexpected pat. "Things will decide themselves, Keeper. They always do." This thought comforted him. He felt better.

Getting out his calendar, the boy began to plan. If he could get to the hidden valley and stay there four or five days, there would be seven weeks left to get to the place where Tío Marco had left him. That is if he got there for Christmas. Christmas would be important to him this year, and that campsite had been an important place. It was there Keeper had accepted him as master, and he had accepted the responsibility of manhood. It would be there, too, that María Cristina would send him the gift she had made for him, the one that Little Mother in faraway Spain had told her how to make. The boy began to mark his calendar.

**26** ACCORDING TO THE MARKINGS on his calendar, they should have reached the place where he and Keeper would turn the mule and the band aside and into an opening between two hills. Through this opening they would reach the hidden valley. Kepa wanted to find the place before Patto-Kak had passed it so as to turn the stubborn mule in the right direc-tion, for the boy knew that where Patto-Kak led, the stupid sheep would follow.

The opening had seemed so easy to find when he had been with the prospector. The two rounded hills with the narrow opening between them had looked different from the ones sur-rounding them but now all the hills looked alike and none of the open places between them was the one he was searching for.

For two days the boy explored the land as the sheep slowly ate their way along. When the band rested, he gave his dog the order to stay and guard them while he walked over the sur-rounding hills looking for tracks of small, sharp hooves on the rocky ground, for bushes that might have been trampled, or broken tree boughs as twenty-five hundred sheep passed by. The stunted plant growth grew low and sturdy. Nothing had damaged them. The juniper and piñon were misshapen and twisted but by the winds of the years, not by a band of sheep in passing.

At last the boy gave up. He had not found the place. They had passed by it.

Midmorning of the third day Kepa walked behind the band that Patto-Kak led and Keeper kept under control. Not having found the hidden valley, they would be days ahead of his planned schedule the boy thought worriedly, wondering if the next night camp would be where he had first met Hans. Then he remembered that because of what had happened to Tío Marco, he had been two days off schedule there. No one herding sheep can make and keep a schedule, he thought disgustedly. A herder is not supposed to think or plan, just follow the sheep trail in and out through the seasons and the years. He picked up a small stone and flicked it at the lazy ewe at the tail end of the band. The stone hit its mark, but the sheep neither raised her head nor changed her pace.

Keeper began to bark, running around the band and nipping the stragglers. Kepa looked to see what was causing the commotion. Patto-Kak was nowhere in sight and slowly, steadily following his lead, the sheep were disappearing too.

The boy ran to the place where the sheep were disappearing and could not believe what he saw. Patto-Kak had known the opening into the hidden valley and was calmly leading the sheep safely into the narrow opening between two rounded hills.

The valley was as the boy remembered it. The water in the creek bed was not frozen into a still line of ice. Now, in November, it babbled over the rocks as merrily as it had in May. The grass was still green. Only the tips of the cottonwood leaves and the willows were rimmed in gold. The air had the warmness of early summer, not the bite of early fall.

Kepa leaned his head against Patto-Kak's shoulder. "My mule, I may be more stubborn than you are, but you are smarter than I am. You found this place, when I had given up." The mule rolled his eyes and flattened his ears, but made no move to kick or bite.

A shrill cackle of laughter made both the boy and mule jump in alarm. "First time I've known a herder to admit his mule is smarter than he is." The little man squatting by the fire stones was shaking with laughter.

"Hans!" Kepa cried in pleased welcome. "Have you been waiting long for me? I'm late, I know."

"I've been long enough to unload my burro and lay a fire. What can you fix to eat? I'm hungry."

"Anything you want," Kepa answered, still laughing in pleasure at the old man's being there. "But first I must unload and water my mule. After my dog, my mule comes first." Then noting that Hans was still laughing at his conversation with Patto-Kak, he said defensively, "This mule leads my band. Can you imagine a mule leading sheep?"

"Often happens," the prospector said. "Sheep will follow anything, even a burro. You're lucky your mule took over."

"I am," Kepa admitted. "I've been hunting for the entrance to this valley for two days. I was worried because I thought I had missed it." The boy got his calendar from his pack. "By my figures on this calendar, we should have been here two days ago."

Hans was unimpressed with the calendar. "I'm for a notched stick to keep track of time," he said. "You can't herd sheep with a stub of a pencil and a scrap of paper. You herd sheep by the feel of it. Got to have a feel for the land and what it offers, a feel for the weather and what it promises. If you have the feel for it you are a shepherd. If you don't you are only a man hired to trail the sheep."

Kepa looked at his shepherd's staff where he had carefully propped it against a tree. "I think I am a shepherd," he said

thoughtfully. "Wherever I'll be, sheep will be part of my life."
Then he laughed, remembering his father's and José's two
flocks, numbering twenty woolly earth-colored creatures.

Kepa watered his mule, pitched his tent, and cooked food for
his dog, his friend, and himself. The old prospector ate swiftly
and silently until his hunger was satisfied. When the food was
gone, he became talkative. "Had two dreams in my life," he
said. "One was a golden dream, a dream of the heart. The other
was a dream of gold, a dream of greed. The second one never
came true. My mind tells me it never will, but something com-
pels me to follow it." The man poured another bowlful of
coffee, put generous amounts of sugar and canned milk into it,
and sipped noisily. Finally he continued talking. "The first
dream never came true either. Years ago I put it away, in the
carved box I showed you, to keep it safe."

Kepa remembered Paco's saying when he gave him the portmanteau that it had held a young man's dreams until he had
found a safer place to put them. Kepa repeated the thought to
Hans, "Until you find a safer place to keep it."

"Already have found it," Hans answered. "You'll know
what I mean, laddie, when the time is right."

Abruptly the prospector changed the subject. "Sheep look
good. Keep them here four, five days to get them ready for
the long trek to the ranch. There is plenty of water and grass
here, but the trail back can be difficult this time of year."

"I won't have any trouble," Kepa told him. "I've been over
the trail before. Besides, now I have only half as many sheep
to care for."

The old man was indignant. "You have as many or more
than you had at first. This time every ewe and yearling in the
band carries two lives, its own and its lamb. It's your responsibility to get them to the lambing sheds in time. From here on in
the trail can be heartbreaking and disastrous."

Kepa thought of what Hans had said about the sheep and the trail on in to the ranch long after he had rolled himself in his blanket for the long night of sleep. He touched his dog curled close beside him. "We'll bring the lambs home safely to be born," he mumbled sleepily.

His dog wakened him in the cold, dark hour before the dawn. It was bitterly cold and night fog lay thickly around him, but the sheep had not wakened. They lay still and undisturbed. "What are you trying to tell me, my friend?" he asked Keeper, looking around the campsite. Hans and his burro were gone. Kepa lit the lantern and made the breakfast fire. On the flat stone beside the burning wood was a small bundle, four goat-skin boots for Keeper's feet.

Eating breakfast, the boy had a heavy feeling of loss as if a friend had gone, a friend whom he would not meet again. After the sun came to light and warmed the valley and his camp chores were done, the boy began to carve. The other carvings he had worked on were hand-sized. This one would be much larger. This one would be a mother bear and her cub, for María Cristina and Christmas.

27 KEPA LOOKED DOWN at the mound that he knew was where Tío Marco's dog lay in his last long sleep. He wondered how Tío Marco was. The last letter Godfather had from the sister in Spain said that Marco was like a little boy again. He had forgotten that he ever had been away from his beloved country. Forty years could be wiped as clean from a person's mind as chalk marks are wiped from a slate. Sensing that his master was worried, the little dog nudged him, and Kepa, as always, responded, talking to him as one would to any friend. "This is the place, Keeper. We got here although we are a day earlier than I planned." Satisfied, the dog ran back to see if the sheep were safe and to tease Patto-Kak by nipping at his heels.

Today was late afternoon, December twenty-second. Kepa had planned to get here tomorrow at this time and stay for Christmas eve and Christmas day. The boy looked around at the plant-starved desert. There would be grazing enough for two days, but not for three. On Christmas morning he must move the band.

He had planned to take seven weeks to get from Hidden Valley to Tío Marco's last campsite. He had done it in about that

174

time, but along the way it had not worked out as he had thought it would. After Hidden Valley, the next camp was where he first had met the old prospector. He knew this was the camp because it had taken a long day to reach it from the valley. Every night or two the boy had made different campsites, but which ones they were he did not know. He had thought he would recognize the site where the coyotes had killed his sheep. But when he reached the place he did not know it. There were coyotes lurking in the shadows of many campsites along the way. He also had thought he would never forget the spot between his bed and his campfire where he had shot the rattle-snake. There were many spots where snakes could coil and lie in wait. Seen for the second time, all the camps looked alike in the bare and empty land that had neither rock nor tree that stood out as special landmarks.

Alberto had come twice with grub and salt and news. He said that they were shorthanded at the ranch. One of the men had gone back to Spain. Carlos had hurt his back and was in town for a week while Godfather Pedro had herded his sheep. Also, he had brought letters; there was one from Little Mother. Father had not been well and they were going to live in the village with Manuel and his wife when he married. "And you, dear son, when you come home," she wrote. The letter gave Kepa much to think about. Of course he was going home. He had known he would go from the beginning, but what would he do in a village in Spain that was little larger than one corral at lambing time in Idaho, America?

There had been one incident along the way that he would remember. He did not remember when it had happened or at what campsite, but toward one evening he had a visitor. A walk-ing, furtive, unarmed man, whose darting glances reminded Kepa of a cornered wild creature crazed with fear. The man was an American, Kepa thought. He spoke English, but in whispered half-formed sentences. He demanded that a sheep be killed and butchered so he could pack it in his hideaway. "You kill it," Kepa yelled at him in his newly learned English, holding his gun ready to use if need be. "You butcher it, you pack it, and then you get out of here." The man did as he was told, wrapping the meat hunks in the sheep pelt and darting into the evening shadows.

Kepa was uneasy. All night he kept guard with his lantern lit, his gun at his hand, and his dog at his feet. Toward dawn he must have dozed, but he was wakened by his dog and his mule and a man's cries of fear and pain.

Taking his gun, Kepa ran with his dog to quiet his mule. Patto-Kak was still short-tempered. He kicked at Keeper and tried to bite Kepa. "He probably tried to steal you, boy," Kepa consoled his mule, "but judging from the spattered blood around, you treated yourself to a big bite." At dawn Kepa followed the bloody tracks a half mile or so, then decided it was wiser to let the thief go and move the sheep.

That was behind him. Who the man was, what happened to him Kepa realized he would never know. His coming and going would be but another incident that the boy could talk about to the old men in Manuel's village in Spain, and the old men would doze while he talked to them and not understand what he was talking about. Kepa remembered the village merchant who had loaned them his mule and his shay to go to San Sebastian. No wonder the man had refused to talk about America. Living memories are alive only to the one who has lived them.

Looking at the landscape again, Kepa knew that on Christmas day he would be trailing his sheep, not waiting by his campfire for the Christmas present María Cristina had made for him. A herder must use what the land offered; his sheep must come first.

Alberto had come a week ago and another week would pass before he would come again. Kepa looked at the food supply.

There still was plenty left. He had learned to balance need against time. "You'll have a feast tonight," he told Keeper. "This is the place where you found yourself." True to his word the boy cooked twice the amount he usually did, but it proved not to be too much. While they were eating Godfather Pedro came riding into camp, leading his pack mule. "Godfather," Kepa called in delight. "It isn't Christmas yet and you have come."

"Well, I had my choice to come Christmas eve or today," Godfather answered, "and I chose today so I could wish you happiness at dawn tomorrow."

Kepa did not understand, "Why tomorrow," he asked.

"Because tomorrow is December twenty-third."

"December twenty-third?" the boy asked, still not understanding. Then his face lighted in pleasure. "My birthday! I had forgotten!"

"Your birthday, your seventeenth," Pedro told him.

"In my eighteenth year," Kepa corrected him.

"In Spain, yes. In America you are seventeen until your eighteenth birthday," Pedro said, laughing. "But it doesn't matter. You are my boy. I saw you first. Seventeen years ago tomorrow, I knew that someday I would give you your chance in America."

Kepa did not answer. He realized, suddenly, how much coming to America meant to him. Even the parts he had not liked were important to him because they had happened to him. If he had not come he would never have known this big, wild, cruel, beautiful land.

To break the silence Pedro said lightly, "I've brought Christmas presents. I'll give them to you tonight—the food packages first because they need to be stored." He handed Kepa a covered basket. "This is from our Little Mother. It's chicken, fish, and cheese. All the Basque goodies you like and seldom can have on the trail."

The boy and the dog looked in the basket and sniffed eagerly. "I hope Keeper and I can save them until it is Christmas," Kepa said, knowing he wanted to eat them now.

"There's enough here," Pedro told him, "for you and your dog to eat steadily from the time I leave in the morning until the end of Christmas day."

"Are you leaving in the morning? You won't be here for Christmas?" Kepa tried to hide his disappointment, but his godfather sensed it. He knew what Christmas meant to a Basque. It was not a day to walk the sheep. He knew. He had experienced it many times. He remembered the poignant loneliness of the trail on Christmas eve and Christmas day.

To hide his emotions his godfather said quickly, "But I'm here for your birthday." He handed a nosebag to the boy. "A special treat. A nosebag of oats for the mule. He'll be more skittish than ever."

"He will be unbearable." Kepa laughed as he put the nose-bag in the tent with the basket of Basque food.

When he came back Godfather Pedro had the pack unloaded. "I might as well give you everything tonight. I am as excited to give them to you as the family was to send them. Son, you mean a lot to my family. Many of the Old World customs get lost between the Basque country and America, but not the family feelings. The families of First Neighbor are as close as kin." Again the boy could find no words to express his happiness, but his look was enough. Pedro said quickly, "Chris made Keeper a leather collar. Not like Tinka's but one more suitable for this little fellow."

Kepa was pleased. He was pleased that Keeper had been remembered and that María Cristina had made it. "It's for you, Keeper," he said, putting the collar around Keeper's neck although he knew that the dog would have preferred a piece of chicken or cheese.

"Here's a special present," Godfather said, handing over a

leather, hand-stitched saddlebag. "The twins made it with help from their mother and Chris and their teacher at school and their scoutmaster and I don't know how many other people. But remember the twins made it. They made it for you."

"It is beautiful. I've been wanting a saddlebag, but I never expected to own one," Kepa said. "Patto-Kak will be proud to carry it, and wouldn't a horse look wonderful with it behind his saddle?"

Pedro untied a cloth-wrapped bundle. "Here is what Chris made for you. Her mother and Rosa helped her with the first ones, but she wasn't satisfied. Chris is a stubborn Basque; she wrote to your mother in Spain for the recipe." The bundle was untied now and Pedro held the present up for Kepa to see. "*Chorizos*," Kepa whispered. "*Chorizos* like Little Mother makes. The last ones she made for me, Alejandro and I ate from San Sebastian to Boise. *Chorizos*," he repeated. "María Cristina made them for me."

"She did," her father boasted proudly. "Worked at them until they tasted right." Then he said worriedly, "Something's the matter with Chris. She cries all the time. I've never known her to cry, even when she broke her arm, but now she cries at nothing."

"María Cristina cries?" Kepa said anxiously. "Maybe she's sick."

"I thought so, too," Godfather admitted, "but her mother said no. Said she was learning that women can be hurt by things they couldn't help. Once she learns, her mother said, she will stop crying and keep her tears in her heart."

"She will?" Again Kepa spoke anxiously.

Pedro nodded. "Most times I feel I know Chris like an open book. Then suddenly I don't understand her at all."

"I know what you mean," Kepa agreed. "Sometimes she's awfully American and then she is completely Basque."

"Well, she's an American Basque," Pedro said as if that explained everything. "If the seven French and Spanish provinces make one, I don't know why the three, Spanish, French, and American Basque, cannot be one."

"They can," Kepa said in surprise. "If seven make one, three make one also." It was a comforting thought. A Basque was a Basque.

After a time of thoughtful silence, Pedro said, "There is one more gift for you. This one is not a Christmas present. It is my gift to the son of my First Neighbor, my godson, my namesake, my new brother-in-law, and my son in the way I feel toward him." Pedro handed Kepa a small square box. The boy opened it with shaking fingers. It could not be, he thought, although it was the size. It was! It was a gold watch like Godfather Pedro had owned so many years ago.

"Godfather . . . Godfather. . . ." He could not say another word.

Pedro spoke hastily. "I forgot. I brought a letter from your mother. Better read it."

Kepa read the short but exciting news. "Luisa has a son," he said, "and they have named it Juan Kepa, for her husband's youngest brother and for me. Wait till I tell Juan," he boasted.

"Juan already knows. Says he's going home for sure, this time to see his namesake."

"He better stay in Idaho," Kepa said severely. "Someone has to give Juan Kepa his chance to come to America."

Later Kepa remembered his own gifts to send back to his godfather's family—the raccoon carving, the rattlers for the twins. Sometime I'll carve them another coyote and maybe I can shoot another rattlesnake, he thought. He had not decided what he would give his godfather, the funny mountain goat or the unfinished mountain lion. Pedro chose the mountain lion. "So you won't go stalking one to find out how to carve his hindquarters," he said, laughing. Kepa had another worry. He did not know what to send Cristina's Little Mother.

180

"She would like kinnekinnick," Pedro said. "Kinnekinnick—
that's the Indian name for them. Sometimes they're called
ground holly. Before I leave in the morning we'll find some of
the little red kinnekinnick berries to take to her. They hide away
under the ground oak."

"Are you sure the Little Mother will like wild berries?"

Pedro started to stay that she would like them very much to
decorate the dinner table on Christmas day, but he stopped himself. No use to turn the knife of loneliness in the boy's heart by
telling him of a Christmas dinner he could not attend because
sheep on the trail needed a herder. He said, "I know she'll like
them very much."

The last present was for María Cristina. It was the mother
bear nosing her baby cub that he had worked on for so long.
Pedro was surprised. "You carved this?" he asked in amazement.
"This is magnificent." Then he said, "Son, don't let carving
steal your heart from the sheep."

"I am a shepherd," Kepa answered him.

"Of a flock in Spain or of a band in America?" Pedro asked.

"I don't know, Godfather. I really do not know."

**28** THERE WERE A FEW DAYS more than six weeks before the sheep would reach the safety of the ranch and the lambing sheds. Kepa planned carefully, using both the calendar and the feel of the land and the weather. The weather was unpredictable, the land he discovered he did not know too well, having been over it only once with Tío Marco. The calendar was his security. Its dates did not change, showing him where he was now and how far he had to go in the time that was left.

Almost all the campsites had to be overnight ones, for the heavy rainy season of the mountain summer had not affected the desert areas. The desert was dry. Many of the water holes of last spring were now only dried scars in the sandy soil. The plant growth was adequate for a day's grazing, and the moisture of the night air gave a day's sufficient water supply, but nothing was in abundance. The sheep had to be kept moving through the warm days, sheltered as best they could be during the cold nights. The wind blew incessantly over the empty land.

Four, five, six weeks went by with the sheep and the herder walking most of the daylight hours. Even the nights were not for undisturbed slumber. Coyotes lurked in the shadows, their hollow laughter made sharper by the low moaning of the night wind.

The sheep were in good condition. There would be a good lamb drop, of that Kepa was certain. His prayer was that he would not lose a lamb. Tío Marco hardly ever had lost a lamb, according to his reputation among the other herders. Kepa was determined to keep to Tío's standard.

Alberto came to leave grub and salt and news. "The Indians say we're going to have a hard winter," he told Kepa. "Better get the sheep as close to the ranch as possible so if snow comes we can get them into the sheds without too great a loss."

"How about Carlos and Juan?" Kepa asked.

"Carlos is dependable. He will get his band in safely." The camp tender laughed. "Juan too, he wants to go home."

"Carlos is dependable. He will get his band in safely," became Kepa's challenge. "I will get my lambs in safely," he repeated as day after day, mile after mile, he walked his sheep ranchward, letting them graze their way to safety.

They were now but two days away. Kepa decided that the campsite they had reached this afternoon had graze enough for tomorrow and they would bed down here another night. The day after he would let Patto-Kak and Keeper lead them triumphantly into the ranch corrals by the lambing sheds.

He took the load from his mule and pitched his tent. He was tired. It had been a steady six-week trek walking the sheep every day with a noonday rest for them and a more or less uneventful night. But now it was behind him. He told Keeper, "This time in two more days you and I and our mule will be at the ranch!"

After they had eaten Kepa put a log on the campfire, a luxury, but tomorrow night there would be no time to sit and dream at a campfire. Tomorrow night they would eat what food was left and pack what they could to help toward an early start the following dawn. Tonight he would sit and think of the year that was past and try to decide what to do in the years ahead. I won't be like Tío or Juan, he thought. I will decide to go and leave America behind me or stay here and only go back to Spain for visits. I cannot, I know, have two worlds, and if I cannot choose between them I will end having neither.

The night was clear with a crescent moon and only a handful of stars. Keeper stretched out between the campfire and his master. The little dog, too, was tired. Kepa tried to make his decision, but he could not force his mind to cope with it. Finally he put another log on the fire, a greater extravagance than the first one had been, and placing his bedroll within its glow curled up inside it, warm and sleepy with Keeper beside him.

He did not know how long he slept, but sometime in the night he was awakened by Keeper's barking and the shrill indignant whinny of his mule. The campfire was still glowing, but clouds hid the moon and stars, and the campsite was gray and shadowy. The boy lit the lantern and, following Keeper, went to find the cause for the alarm. A ewe was in trouble, seemingly in pain, but there was no wound and no enemy crouching in the shadow. Kepa walked among the sheep, but Keeper did not go with him. The sheep were restless, uneasy, but they did not scatter or mill.

The boy went back to the ewe in trouble. Keeper stood guarding it. In the dim lantern light Kepa discovered a newborn lamb. Looking closer he discovered another one. "No, no," he wailed, "Not twin lambs." He looked at them in panic. The past summer had been an exceptionally good one for grazing and water, which he knew often resulted in an exceptionally high birthrate of twin lambs.

The boy worked for a long time with the young ewe, but he could not save her. Was it because he did not know what should have been done? Was it because he had no experience that he

184

had let her suffer and finally die? He raged, looking at the animal that was now beyond his help. Finally, he made himself look at the lambs she had given her life to bear. They seemed strong enough to live, if he could get them dry, get them warm, and feed them with some substitute for their mother's milk.

Kepa warmed his blanket at his campfire. What had prompted him, he wondered, to keep a fire burning through the night. He took a warm stone that had made a part of the wall of his fireplace, put it in the folds of his blanket and wrapped it around the newborn lambs. The boy heated canned milk, diluted it with water, and drop by drop dripped it into the small hungry mouths. At last the cold, wet, orphaned babies were dry. At last they were warm. At last they were sleeping.

As he had worked with the lambs Kepa had been aware of his dog's actions. Keeper had run to him, disappeared into the shadows at the campsite's edge, then ran back to his master again and disappeared again. The boy remembered his mule's whinny, which had helped waken him. Not coyotes, not bobcats, he thought. Not in the same night with my first experience of helping lambs get born. This can't happen to a herder!

Taking his gun, he cautiously followed Keeper into the shadows. Before him stood a small, dejected burro and beneath the burro's body lay Hans. Kepa bent over him. The old man was alive; he was conscious. He was talking incoherently and clutching the carved wooden box tightly in his clawlike hands. The boy half carried, half dragged the hairy little man to the campfire. He got the blanket from the burro pack, warmed it and wrapped it snugly around the little gnome creature. Then Kepa made coffee, hot and strong, and coaxed the man to drink it.

Revived, Hans began to talk. "Came back, laddie, to tell you . . . the end of my trail . . . wanted to tell you." A spasm of coughing stopped him. Kepa gave him more coffee, drop by drop, which reminded him of how he had fed the lambs. After a time, the old man began to talk again. "You and the lassie . . . make my dream come true . . . together . . . open the box . . . it's in the box." The old prospector stopped talking. He had said what he had come to say, almost all that he had come to say.

Kepa propped the old man against his packsaddle. He will rest even if he can't sleep, the boy thought, and went to see if the lambs still lived. They were baaing hopelessly, teetering on the thin line between life and death. Kepa warmed them again, fed them, and watched sleep enfold them, then went back to old Hans who again was talking. "Gretchen loved me." Kepa bent closer to him. This was something he had to know.

"How did you know Gretchen loved you?" he asked intently. "How does anyone know someone loves him?" He had to know the answer.

The prospector opened his eyes for a heartbeat of time. "Be-cause she was good to me . . . in little things . . . in things of the heart." His voice faltered. "But I . . . didn't . . . appreciate . . . I lost her. . . ." So that was the answer, Kepa thought. Love was doing little things for the one you loved. He thought of the *chorizos*.

**29** DAWN WAS BREAKING through a cloudy sky. Kepa cooked breakfast but only Keeper ate. It began to snow, big, slow flakes that turned and turned and at last fell softly upon the ground.

He decided to move the band to the safety of the ranch. If he started now he could reach the ranch before nightfall. He tried to rouse old Hans, who was now lying against the packsaddle, but could get no response. The only strength the old man showed was in his clutching of the carved wooden box.

The boy warmed and fed the lambs again, put the pack load on the mule, the lambs into his Christmas saddlebag, which he tied securely on the load. He was ready to go and, giving the order to Keeper, the band began to move.

Kepa picked up the old prospector, draped him around his shoulders in the same way that he once carried a lamb and later a dog, and began trudging through the snow. The snow fell faster and more thickly, covering the ground as the mule and his load, the sheep, the burro, the dog, and the shepherd bearing his burden moved on.

How many hours and miles he walked Kepa never knew. Like the snow-filled land, the twisted trees and stunted bushes were lost in swirling snow, and so was time, distance, and conscious thought.

The boy's heart beat faster, thumping, pushing against the pain in his chest, but he was not conscious of either heart flutter or pain. Neither was he conscious that his mind was commanding his feet to step forward, one step at a time, one more step, carefully and steadily, even-paced . . . don't stumble . . . don't fall . . . don't dare to stop to rest . . ." Under his burden his back stiffened and shoulders ached, but he did not falter. The pain in his chest flowed upward, filling his throat, leaving him panting and gasping for breath, but he followed his brain's command automatically . . . one step at a time . . . one more step. Silently the snowflakes fell as soft as the down of baby birds. Snow swirled about the boy's body, clinging to his clothing, matting his eyelashes, blurring his vision, but still he trudged on.

Suddenly something stopped him. Angrily, he tried to push forward, mumbling, "I can't stop . . . I must not stop."

"Kepa, Kepa," a voice kept shouting, as Hans was lifted from his shoulders. "Kepa, Kepa!" At last the voice cut through the fog that clouded the boy's brain. Kepa stared vacantly, trying to focus his sight and senses on the three people standing before him. He asked uncertainly, "Godfather Pedro . . . the twins?" Then as reality came back to him, he said, "Godfather Pedro . . . somewhere inside me I knew for sure that you would come."

"I came, son," Pedro said quietly. Are you all right?"

"Yes, but Hans? What have you done with Hans and the lambs? They were still living a while ago."

"They are alive and so is Hans," his godfather answered. He began giving orders to the twins. "The two of you are to ride to the ranch as fast as you can go. Tommy, you take the lambs to Rosa at the ranch. She can save them if anyone can. Tony, tell Ramón to warm up the lambing shed he has for Kepa. Tell him to have all the stoves red hot."

So, Kepa thought, the twins do have names, even if they are seldom used. Suddenly, he remembered what they were, Tomás and Antonio. Tommy and Tony, he supposed, were the English way of saying them.

Godfather was still talking to the twins. "Then both of you go home. Tell your mother and Chris to drive the car as far as the snowplow has cleared the road. They are to wait for me there. I'll be bringing Hans for them to take home."

"May we come back with them in the car?" the twins asked.

"No. Stay in Boise. Have the doctor waiting for Hans when your mother and Chris bring him." Then gently, he said to them, "They will need you. I cannot be there, you must take my place."

"Where will you be . . . at the ranch?" the twins asked.

"I will go to the ranch, pick up a fresh horse and come back to help Kepa."

"We are going . . . you can depend on us," the twins answered.

Kepa watched them ride away. Now his godfather was speaking to him. "Help me load Hans on the back of my saddle. It's a good thing this horse rides double." This accomplished, the man put his hands on Kepa's shoulder. "Keep the sheep moving. If this snow keeps us they'll be dropping lambs on the trail. You must reach the lambing shed as soon as possible. Son, can you do it alone? It will be hours before I can get back."

Kepa grinned. "Godfather, remember? Remember I'm a stubborn Basque?"

"We are all stubborn Basque or we wouldn't be here," Pedro answered, turning his horse toward the ranch. That was what Alberto had said, Kepa remembered. The words comforted him and gave him courage.

The boy watched his godfather, with Hans, ride into the storm, and he remembered the time that Pedro had taken Tío from the sheep camp. Godfather always comes when we need him, the boy thought. Hans will be all right now that God-father has him. Tío is fine now. Hans will be too. The thought helped him, and knowing that his godfather would return to be with him was also a comfort. He called to his dog to hurry the sheep along. They must reach the ranch as quickly as possible.

Noontime came and passed. Keeper kept the band moving. The sheep would not have rested in such a storm, and much more important to Kepa than rest or food was getting the ewes to the lambing shed before more lambs were born.

In midafternoon he found a ewe in trouble. Giving the signal to Keeper to keep the band moving, the boy stayed behind to help the mother deliver her baby, but the lamb was dead. He could do nothing to revive it. Almost immediately he found a dead ewe and a newborn lamb. Kepa knew what to do; he had not seen it done but Tío Marco had told him how to do it. Awkwardly skinning the yellow-stained, woolly pelt from the dead lamb, he sewed it, coatlike, around the orphaned living one. Gently, timidly, he edged the young orphan beside a bleat-ing ewe that was searching in vain for her newborn baby. Breathlessly the boy stood over the ewe and the lamb. The ewe sniffed it cautiously, nudged it, then accepted it as her lamb. The scent was right.

A deep surge of happiness warmed the wet, half-frozen boy as he looked down on a contented ewe and a nuzzling lamb. He turned as his godfather put a hand on his shoulder. "Well done, son," Pedro said quietly.

"Godfather, I didn't hear you come."

"I know, you were too busy."

Together the man and the boy watched the ewe and her accepted newborn. "I did it!" Kepa exclaimed in amazement. "I fixed it so she thinks the lamb belongs to her. It gives me a wonderful feeling, Godfather Pedro."

Again Pedro said, "I know," and added, "This is sheep busi-ness. Sheep business has its exalted moments."

190

In late afternoon snow stopped falling and the sun came out from behind its curtain of snow cloud. Patto-Kak led his band of bleating sheep through the ranch gates as the setting sun, for a brief few minutes, clothed the snow-covered western hills in crimson light.

The long lambing shed was warm from the heat of the big pot-bellied stoves at each end and in the middle. The ewes were herded into their separate pens, each pen with clean, fresh straw and large enough for a ewe, one or two lambs, and, if need be, one of the men who were hired to attend the sheep at lambing times.

Kepa waited until all the sheep were bedded and his own small lamb asleep by its new mother. Then he went to the ranch-house kitchen to ask Rosa about the lambs the twins had brought her.

The welfare of the lambs was forgotten when Rosa told him as gently as she could that Hans had died an hour ago. The boy could not believe her. "But Godfather Pedro took him. He has to be all right because he was with Godfather Pedro," he kept saying. Rosa answered all his questions. Yes, Chris and her mother had brought the car as far as they could. Pedro had met them there. They had taken Hans to their home in Boise where the doctor was waiting for them, but Hans had died. Chris's mother had phoned the ranch that Hans had died an hour ago.

There was silence. Then Rosa said, perhaps to comfort herself, "He died in bed. At least he didn't have to die by the side of the trail." Again Kepa did not answer, but he wondered if dying in bed had comforted Hans. Perhaps the old man would have wanted to die as he had lived—by the side of the trail.

"Chris was with him every minute," Rosa said. "The old man told her things he wanted her to know." Still Kepa could find no words to answer her. Rosa continued. "She is taking it very hard, her mother said. The doctor is with her. Her mother is worried about her." Then Rosa added, "Poor little Chris."

Kepa turned and left the ranch house. "Chris needed me," he said fiercely to himself. "All that time that she was needing me I was walking the sheep on the trail."

The boy went to the bunkhouse, not to sleep but to lie dry-eyed through the slow-moving hours. He had never told Hans how much he had taught him. Hans would never know how much he had guided him. "Now he is dead," the boy said. "Hans is dead."

**30** LAMBING SEASON WAS OVER. It had been a busy but profitable one. In the three bands more than four thousand lambs had been born and almost four thousand lambs had lived. The sun was sparkling and warm, only patches of snow were left as reminders of the recent storm. The herders had been paid and had gone to Boise to celebrate the ending of the sheepman's year. Juan had gone with the others to buy his ticket to go to Spain, but Ramón said laughingly his extra clothes were still in the bunkhouse. Carlos and the other men hired to take care of the ewes and the newborn lambs remained at the ranch. The men because there was work for them to do and Carlos because he liked staying at the ranch. He was content to stay there while his companions went shouting into town. He hated towns, all towns, and he liked Rosa's cooking.

Kepa had been the last one in to the lambing sheds and therefore was the last one to be called to the little office by the bunkhouse, where Pedro paid the men what was due them for their long year's work. Pedro looked tired. His face was drawn and strained, but he had his usual smile for his godson. "Sit down, son. This should not take long." The man waited until the boy was seated beside his desk, then abruptly he said, "You know Hans died?"

Kepa nodded. "Rosa told me."

"I loved him as I loved my father," Pedro said quietly. "I loved that old man."

Kepa tried to comfort him. "The old man knew he was going to die," he said. "I guess he was ready to go."

"He was ready," Pedro answered. Then he said, "Chris and her mother did all they could for him. Chris was with him when he died. Her mother would have stayed but Hans wanted Chris alone." Pedro looked at the boy sitting quietly by his desk. "Chris is taking this very hard. She seems to have many sorrows and I cannot help her." The man looked down at the account book open before him. He was a Basque. It is difficult for a Basque to bare his heart. Finally he said, "These things happen. A man is born; he dies." Kepa nodded. They understood one another, Pedro and Kepa. This was their benediction for a loved one who was gone. Finally, Pedro smiled at the boy, and asked, "Are you ready, son, to go over your accounts?" Kepa returned his smile and nodded. "Well then, here they are. This is what you earned. This column is what you owe for the things we bought for you. You spent very little. This is the amount left over. It is a sizeable amount."

"You haven't charged me for my passage over," Kepa said, reading the figures.

"No, remember I told you—I pay your way over, you pay it back."

"Yes," Kepa said, "you did tell me that."

"Well, it's settled then. I owe you this amount."

"I want to send some of it to my mother and father and to my brother Manuel."

Pedro looked at him. "Did you say you want to send it or did you say you want to take it?"

"I said I want to send it. I am not going back to Spain. I am staying here. I want to become a sheepman like you."

194

Pedro went to the window of the little office and looked out into the dazzling sunshine at the woolly newborn lambs playing in their corrals. Finally, he said, "I can't tell you what this means to me, son. This is what I've wanted for seventeen years." He came back to the desk. "If you want sheep, you should start getting a few now and keep adding to them. You can run them with my band. We'll talk about that this evening. Chris and the twins are waiting to take you in to the house in Boise. I guess the twins are with her. I heard her mother tell her to take them."

Kepa started to leave but his godfather stopped him. "What made you decide to stay?" he asked.

Kepa was embarrassed. He tried to form an answer. Finally he said, "Well . . . a lot of things, I guess. There was Hans' death . . . and the mother sheep and her orphan lamb, and, you know, being needed . . . and *chorizos* are difficult to make. They take a lot of work."

Pedro looked blank. "Do you want to say all that again?"

Kepa tried again. "Hans died. . . ." He stopped.

"I know," Pedro said, "but you were telling me why you decided to stay."

"Oh? Well, once Hans told me something about not appreciating something until after you had lost it," he answered vaguely.

His godfather seemed to understand. "That reminds me," he said, "here is the carved box. Hans gave it to Chris, but she said for me to give it to you. You would know what Hans wanted to be done with it."

"I know," Kepa told him, taking the box. "I know what Hans wants done with it."

The boy went out to the car where Chris was waiting for him. He was shocked when he saw her. She looked sick. The boy stood awkwardly by the car, wanting to say something, but not knowing what to say.

195

"Carlos put your things in the trunk. Keeper is with the other dogs," Chris told him. "I'm taking you home with me."

"Where are the twins?" Kepa asked.

"Where they should be, at school," Chris answered shortly. "We'll pick them up on the way home. Get in." Chris started the car and they drove in silence.

Kepa said, "I'm sorry about Hans. I did all I could."

"I know," Chris answered. "We all did all we could."

The road was dry and smooth. It seemed to Kepa that they were going very fast. Chris neither spoke nor looked at him. Finally Kepa said, "Will you keep Hans' box for me?"

The car swerved. Chris kept her gaze steadily on the road before her as she answered him. "I will keep the box," she said slowly, "and also your dog, if you want me to keep him."

"My dog?" Kepa shouted. "Why should you keep my dog?"

"Someone has to keep him when you go home to Spain."

Kepa shouted again, but this time with laughter. "I'm not going to Spain. I'm going to stay here and become a sheepman like Godfather. He says he thinks I can get my start in about four years. Tina," he said. It was the first time he had called her anything shorter than Cristina. "Tina, how long will it take you to finish school?"

"About four years," she answered. Suddenly she looked at him. "Did Hans tell you what to do with the box?" she asked.

"Did he tell you?" Kepa wanted to know.

"Yes."

"That we should open it together?" he asked.

"Yes."

"All right," Kepa said softly, "that's what we will do. In the aspen grove."

"By the waterfall." They both laughed. "We're talking like the twins," Chris said.

"Because we think alike," Kepa finished.

196

They had reached the twins' school. "We pick them up here," Chris explained, stopping the car. Her face was alight with happiness. "Now you can buy a horse, so you won't have to walk the trails."

"Buy a horse?" Kepa was horrified. "Horses cost money. I need every penny I can earn to get started with my band, and until I get started I will walk the trails like your father did."

Chris said softly, "You, like my father did, will walk the trails and I, like my mother did, will cry because you walk them."

The twins came running from the school building. "How come you bring Kepa to get us?" one twin shouted furiously, and the other one, also furious, added, "You knew our mother told you that we were to go with you to get Kepa."

"But this is the way it happened," Kepa said. "I hope you understand."

There was a second of silence. Then they both spoke together, and meekly, "We understand."

*About the Author*

ANN NOLAN CLARK was born in Las Vegas, New Mexico, and served for many years as a teacher and writer
for the Bureau of Indian Affairs, the State Department, and the
Department of Education in Latin America. She has written
numerous books about children in different parts of the world,
including *In My Mother's House*, a Caldecott Honor Book,
and *The Secret of the Andes*, set in Peru, which won the New-
bery Award. In 1963 Mrs. Clark received the Regina Medal
from the Catholic Library Association for "continued distin-
guished contributions to literature for children."

Mrs. Clark gathered the material for *Year Walk* on two
trips to Spain and several visits to the sheep-raising regions of
Idaho. She now lives in a small desert town outside Tucson,
Arizona.